P9-DOC-181

DOG DRIVEN

3 1526 05350754 4

WITHDRAWN

DOG DRIVEN

By Terry Lynn Johnson

HOUGHTON MIFFLIN HARCOURT
BOSTON   NEW YORK

Copyright © 2019 by Terry Lynn Johnson

All rights reserved. For information about permission to reproduce selections
from this book, write to trade.permissions@hmhco.com or to Permissions,
Houghton Mifflin Harcourt Publishing Company, 3 Park Avenue, 19th Floor,
New York, New York 10016.

hmhbooks.com

The text was set in Bembo Book MT Std.

Map artwork by Keith Robinson

Library of Congress Cataloging-in-Publication Data
Names: Johnson, Terry Lynn, author.
Title: Dog driven / by Terry Lynn Johnson.
Description: Boston ; New York : Houghton Mifflin Harcourt, [2019] |
Summary: McKenna, fourteen, is losing her vision to Stargardt's disease, but that
will not stop her from competing in a rigorous new sled dog race through the
Canadian wilderness.
Identifiers: LCCN 2018026339 | ISBN 9781328551597 (hardcover)
Subjects: | CYAC: Dogsledding — Fiction. | Sled dogs — Fiction. | Dogs — Fiction. |
People with visual disabilities — Fiction. | Wilderness areas — Fiction. |
Survival — Fiction. | Ontario — Fiction. | Canada — Fiction.
Classification: LCC PZ7.J63835 Dog 2019 | DDC [Fic] — dc23
LC record available at https://lccn.loc.gov/2018026339

Printed in the United States of America
DOC 10 9 8 7 6 5 4 3 2 1
4500777713

To the Stargardt disease community, for your support

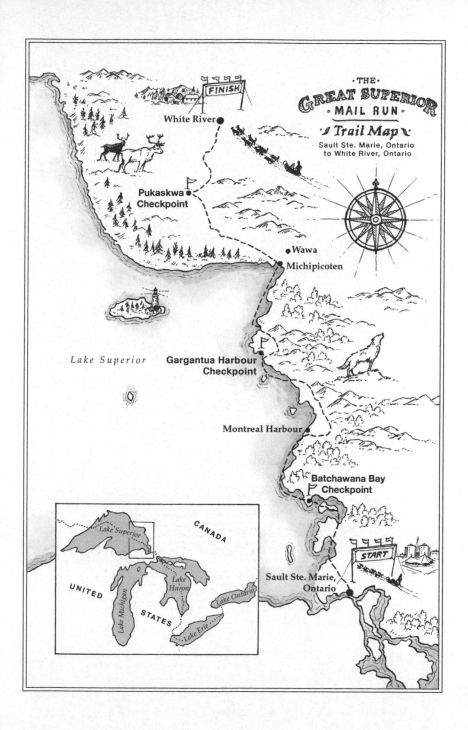

·THE·
GREAT SUPERIOR
· MAIL RUN ·
↝ Trail Map ↜
Sault Ste. Marie, Ontario
to White River, Ontario

FINISH

White River

Pukaskwa
Checkpoint

Wawa
Michipicoten

Lake Superior

Gargantua Harbour
Checkpoint

Montreal Harbour

Batchawana Bay
Checkpoint

START

Sault Ste. Marie,
Ontario

CANADA

Lake Superior

UNITED

Lake Michigan

Lake
Huron

Lake Ontario

STATES

Lake Erie

CHAPTER 1

Whoever's behind me is coming fast.

I peek over my shoulder and see a blurry line of shapes bearing down. Mustard glances back too, then faces forward and digs in. He's so cocky. He hates getting passed.

An unspoken message travels through the whole team and they surge forward together. I love how the speed comes up through my feet. Cold air darts through cracks in my neck warmer. I squint into the wind.

"Gee over, Mustard. Don't be rude. Attagirl, Twix."

I have an eight-dog team, so my front-runners are at the edge of my visual range. All I can see of my leaders are furry shapes. It's as though my sunglasses are coated in Vaseline. The bright sun compounds the issue. When it reflects off the snow, it hurts my eyes, even with my dark shades.

The sound of synchronized panting grows louder behind me.

"Trail!" a boy's voice calls.

I have just enough time to angle my sled to the right before his dogs come loping up beside me. They move along my sled, then shoulder past it to my dogs.

Saga and Haze both stick their faces directly in the way, stretching their necks for a good sniff. I cringe. Sixteen dogs running this close beside one another at ten miles an hour can make a nice tangled ball in a blink.

"Ahead!" I call, trying to keep the embarrassment out of my voice. Why can't my dogs behave like everyone else's when we're out in public? I'm driving savages. I watch the other team. Focused ahead, no nonsense, passing like pros.

I stare at the musher as he glides by. He's near my age, or maybe a little older. And he's wearing some kind of war uniform that looks like it came out of his great-grandfather's closet.

"Ma'am," he says. He doesn't even watch his dogs to make sure they're going straight, just turns backwards on the runners and bows at me. *Bows.*

"Hey, Retro," I call. "Why bother? Now I'm going to have to pass you!"

He laughs and then he's out of my range, leaving me with the sounds of the trail—the *shush* of the runners gliding over sun-softened snow, then the clacking noise they make on the harder, shaded sections of trail. The necklines tinkle, and the wind whistles. I could never run this fast on my own. Never feel the clean bite of air filling up my nostrils. Filling *me* up.

I'm never as free as I am out here behind this team.

My gaze roves up and down my dogs. Sumo's dipping snow already but keeping pace. The fluorescent strips I've stitched along the backs of the dog harnesses make them stand out, especially on white dogs like Damage and Haze. Without the strips I can hardly tell them from a snowbank. But the real trouble will start at dusk, when everything turns into black blobs, fluorescent strips or not.

A wide-open expanse appears. My team goes down the bank and then moves onto the frozen lake. There's a commotion ahead; I hear it before I see it. Two mushers, yelling.

"Grab your leaders!"

"Sorry! I'm sorry!"

Dogs barking.

Their teams flounder in the snow. I arrive just as the dogfight breaks out. I throw down my snow hook, wondering what to do next. Should I go help? No, I'll surely give myself away, stumbling over dogs.

My team shrieks and lunges to get closer to the action. I'm hesitant to leave the sled in case Sumo pops the hook and we have three teams tangled. But I can't tell what's going on from back here. I creep closer, moving up beside my leaders. The mushers are grabbing armfuls of dogs and tugs.

"They wouldn't listen!" A girl wearing yellow wind pants struggles with a dog as if she's never untangled a dog team before.

"What are you doing?" It's the retro boy who passed me. "Unclip the tug or my dog will get pinched!"

"This one?"

"No, your point dog! Hurry! Yoda, enough!"

His wheel dog, not even in the tangle, is screaming so loud now, it's hard for me to think. Which is why I dive into the fray.

I reach for the girl's leggy point dog, flicking off my mitts as I do so my bare fingers are ready. Once I've grabbed the dog, I go by instinct. Unclip the tug, flip the line under, then reclip her dog. It's all automatic and takes about two seconds.

The line is still tangled.

I walk backwards a few steps with the tugs, straightening the leaders, and squint at the gangline. There. A neckline needs to be unclipped. Once I've got the leaders untangled, I have to hold the leggy dog's collar to prevent him from turning around. It's satisfying to know that my dogs aren't the worst brats ever.

I peer at my team but can see only a line of crazed, hopping mongrels. I'm too far away to tell if the snow hook is coming loose. *Please don't come loose.*

My feet sink through the crust of snow and I slop around in slush. "You want to get them going," I tell the girl. "I'll hold them out."

She seems to suddenly come out of her fog and leaps onto her sled.

"Hike up!" she yells, and the dogs pitch forward, picking up speed. Her sled zips past me, throwing up a rooster tail of slush.

"Thanks," the boy says. "I think she's new."

I feel a nose shoving at my butt. I turn and recognize the black and silver markings of the boy's lead dog. But then I do a double take and peer closer. Her eyes! "What's wrong with your dog?"

"What?" The boy looks up, then relaxes. "Oh, you mean Zesty. Yeah, she's blind as a bat. Anyway, thanks for your help."

"You . . . your lead dog . . . you have a *blind* lead dog?"

"She's the best. Hey, love to chat, but should we get going? You know. *Race.*"

I peer intently into Zesty's face. She's focused on the departing team, ears erect, body tightly coiled. She appears to be watching, but her eyes are fully clouded over. She swivels her face toward me as if sensing I'm staring.

"Your team!"

I jerk my gaze up. The boy lunges for my sled as it shoots past him. His feet get bogged down in the slush. He misses.

I have one chance. I try to line myself in the right place but it's going to be tight. I can't see the sled clearly, and my depth perception is off. How close is it? Where is that handlebar? My dogs rush past me as I lean over, desperate, reaching . . . reaching.

Bam!

My bent arm hooks the handlebar. I swing up onto the runners. Step on the brake. Lean down to where the snow hook should be. There it is. Snag it up. Set it in its cradle. Straighten, focus ahead. Adrenaline still pumping.

I can feel my dogs smiling from here.

I told him I'd pass him.

December 7, 1896

Dear Margaret,

I leave the port of Killarney on the morrow with the mail courier Raymond Miron and his team of dogs. There is wild beauty here with windswept pines and stark white cliffs, but also loneliness. I miss home terribly. Alas, the Hudson's Bay Company requires me at White River upon the most haste, and I shall endeavor to comply . . .

Love to little Anna. She will be grown enough to beat me in a horserace when I return.

Your loving brother, William

CHAPTER 2

Two months before the race

I open the puppy pen's metal door with a creak, and our three yearlings from last year's litter explode past me.

Their frenetic energy rarely fails to cheer me up, but this time I stand next to the pen, a shovel in hand, and peer at the door in dismay.

When we first built the pen, Mom painted BARNEY KENNELS in bright red across the door. Though it's faded now, the letters are still stark against the pattern of dog-paw prints she'd added in blue. It's the same pattern as the trim in my little sister's old bedroom. I've always been jealous of it. The trouble is, I can no longer see the pattern.

For the past few months I've let myself believe that perhaps I just need glasses. Glasses or something else, maybe corrective surgery, and I'll be all fixed. However, living with Emma, I know the signs.

Last month, I could still see the pattern. Today, it has slipped behind a spot in the center of my vision. I close one eye. The little off-center patch in my vision has grown over the past few weeks. It's slightly purple and distorted, like when you press on your eyeball and see sparkles. When I open that eye and close the other one, the spot moves. I open both eyes, and the spot now meets in the center of my vision. I've been tracking where the distorted spot appears. Up to now, when both eyes were open, I could still see in the center. It's happened so fast. And because of how fast it happened, I know.

I clutch the smooth wooden handle of the shovel. There is no denying it any longer. I have it. A hot bubble of fear and grief swells inside me. *How can I live with this?*

I hear Mom and Emma pulling into the driveway. "I'm in the yard," I call out, eager for a distraction.

"McKenna! Oh my God!" Em's voice, quivering with excitement. "You'll never guess!"

"The yearlings are loose!" I warn Mom as the pups thunder past me.

Emma comes into view, holding on to the crook of Mom's

arm as they make their way to me. Em's not even bothering with her cane. Again.

The yearlings turn and gallop back, biting each other's necks, not looking where they're going. But they somehow avoid plowing into my sister and continue on a loop around the fence line.

I wait till Emma comes close. "Good day at school?" I ask.

"There's gonna be a new dogsled race in Canada, McKenna! It's called the Great Superior Mail Run," Emma says, speaking quickly as she releases her grip on Mom. "Mushers carry real mail in their sleds so it gets stamped with DELIVERED BY DOG TEAM on it! And guess what—our class is going to write letters! They can be to anyone."

"That sounds cool," I say.

The yearlings arrive at my feet in a pile, growling and mock fighting. They have the whole dog yard to run around in, but apparently they need an audience. Their faces are covered in one another's goober, which is beginning to freeze stiff like hair gel. Suddenly they leap up and go tearing off again full throttle.

Emma giggles as she turns her head to the side to see them. "I bet if I wrote the Foundation for Fighting Blindness and asked them for more research on Stargardt disease, they'd *have* to do it. It would stand out from all the other mail with the stamp on it. I mean, duh, right? And then I bet it'll be on TV. Everyone would hear about Stargardt's and want to donate money for research."

It's my sister's simple view of the world. The research for a cure needs to be done, so everyone should care about it.

"Right." I glance at Mom uneasily. I hope this isn't going where I think it's going.

"And they'd for sure put it on TV when they find out it's my *sister* who's delivering it!" Em waves her arms around like a dork, flapping her fleece gloves, and I have to smile despite the dread that's lodged in my gut.

I look to Mom again, grasping for a lifeline, but she has no idea what's going on with me. She nods as if to say of course I'm racing it. I realize they've already talked about this and now I'm ambushed.

"The dogs would love a stage race like this," Mom says. "You've run them so much this season, they're in top form. And it's a great idea to help your sister. We could all use a bit of hope, don't you think, McKenna?"

Mom takes my shovel. She's trying to bridge the gap of silence that's grown between us lately, but I don't know how to cross it. There's an awkward little moment when our eyes meet, but then I look away. She sighs and starts cleaning the yard where I left off.

"But they wouldn't let the junior mushers carry the mail," I say — and then almost get knocked off my feet from behind when two of the three nerds barrel into the backs of my legs. "Watch it!"

"That's the perfect part," Emma says. "This race is open to mushers fourteen and up, so you'll just make it! Juniors race with adults!"

Em carefully takes the two steps to Sumo's doghouse and leans her butt against it. She claps softly, and the big dog rests his chin on her thigh. I have no idea how he knows not to jump up on her, but it's probably the reason she adores him. He's a gentle giant. Until he's running in the team — then he's a steam engine.

Emma continues. "The race is like a celebration of dogsledding because they used to bring stuff to the towns by dog team. It's important to history. That's why my teacher wants us to be part of it. She said the Canadian dogsled mail run was like the Pony Express here in the States. Can you believe it? Everyone in my class was talking about how amazing dogsledding is!"

And there's the reason she wants me to run it. Because she can't. Suddenly, all her friends are interested in dogsledding, and wouldn't it be great if she were the star of her class for once? My heart cracks.

You'd think for someone who gets everything done for her, she'd be bratty. But that's the thing about Em. She's so sweet that it makes you want to do things for her all the time. She's not like most kids her age. Maybe because she's been through so much crap already. Hardship makes you tough. She doesn't take kindness for granted or expect stuff from people, like big gifts or trips to Disney.

Since she was young when the symptoms began, only six, it took a while to get the diagnosis from the retina specialist. I can never forget that visit when we were told what it was. Having so many different tests in one day traumatized my whole family. And in the two years since then, her disease has quickly worsened.

She has some sight. Most people don't know there are levels of sight impairment. Her last exam showed she's 20/600, worse than last year, when she was 20/200, which is legally blind. I hate that it's labeled like that because it's so confusing. She's not *blind* just because she can't see that stupid letter at the top of the eye chart anymore. She can see better in her peripheral vision.

Before I started worrying about crashing, I used to take her out with me in my sled all the time because she made it so fun. Her excitement over the wind in her face, the motion of going fast. She would love to be able to mush a team on her own. But she can't run like she used to. She only has me to run her dogs for her.

Mom corrals the yearlings back into the pen and looks up at

the house. "Are you okay, Emma?" She asks this question about fifteen thousand times a day.

"Yeah, Mom."

I'm standing right here, but still Mom hesitates to leave Emma. "Well, if you're sure, I'll see you inside." She rubs Emma's arm. To me she says, "We'll talk over the details at dinner, okay? I'm going to get it ready. Watch your sister."

Em turns to me expectantly and my mind spins. How could I enter this race? I can't run on trails I don't know. It's dangerous enough running my own trails where I remember all the corners. Even running here is getting worse. Painful when it's too sunny out. And now that I know for sure what I have . . .

What if there are low-hanging branches on the race trails that I don't see in time? What if there's a bad hill? I could roll off a cliff. I could lose the team. I could hit a tree and break my collarbone like Keith Scott last year. I could fall off, break a leg, break my teeth, get dragged, get Mustard hurt. I could get us all lost! How easy would it be to miss the trail markers and flounder around alone on unblazed, unsafe trails?

And all of that is if the weather and trail conditions are perfect. What if there's a storm? Icy sections of trail? There's just no way I can run a team on unknown trails.

I could get us all *killed*.

Em is still waiting, hopeful. Me being six years older makes her think I can do anything. I want to give her anything. I want to give her the stars. I want to give her her sight back.

But I can't do this.

DECEMBER 11, 1896

DEAR MARGARET,

WE ARE HAVING A STRENUOUS TIME ON THE LAKE ICE, ENDURING THE IMMENSE COLD THAT SEEPS INTO ONE'S BONES. THE WIND IS INCESSANT. I AM GRATEFUL THAT WE ARE SHARING THE WIGWAMS OF THE OJIBWE AS WE WERE DRENCHED THROUGH FROM SLUSH AFTER WRESTLING WITH THE SLEIGH. SWIFT WATER LURKS UNDERNEATH THE SNOW IN PLACES. BUT DO NOT FRET; MY COMPANION IS EXCEEDINGLY KNOWLEDGEABLE ABOUT WHERE TO STEP.

YOUR LOVING BROTHER, WILLIAM
A POSTSCRIPT: PLEASE DO NOT TELL ANNA ABOUT HER UNCLE FREEZING HALF TO DEATH.

CHAPTER 3

E m," I begin. "I . . . I'm too busy with school right now to focus on a big race like that. I've got tests coming up and assignments. And I've got that project on ancient Egypt I haven't even started."

She makes a rude noise that surprises me. "Yeah, right."

I see that's not going to fly. "I'm not even in shape. You know I quit the running team. I'll cough up a lung. It could actually happen."

"The dogs are in shape."

"I've never run the trails up there. I might get lost."

"You didn't get lost running the UP Midnight Run last year," she points out.

"Em . . . I can't do it. I'm sorry."

Emma grows serious. The hope slips from her face. "Why not?"

I owe her something. And not an excuse; she's too smart. What am I going to tell her? The seconds tick by. She's going to figure it out if I don't say something. She knows more than anyone how it feels to have this. Maybe I should be honest with her. Adrenaline surges through me at the thought. I swore to myself *no* one would know.

My voice is limp. "I . . . I've been having some trouble . . . with my vision."

"*What?* Why didn't you tell me? What can you see? Do you think it's Stargardt's? But the doctor said your eyes are clear. They've always been clear! You need to get tested right away. We have to tell Mom and Dad!" Her words are rapid gunfire.

I panic. "No! No, no, we're not telling them. It's not as bad as yours. It's just a bit of blurriness in the sun. I didn't tell you because there's almost nothing to tell." Everything is happening too fast. I haven't even processed the fact that I have it too. I don't have a plan yet besides keeping it from my parents at all costs. I have to stay independent.

"No! You have to tell them now! You could hurt yourself!"

Her face is full of heartbreak and scares me more than

anything. It's always been a possibility in my mind, this thing I might have. But now with it out in the open, especially with Em, who knows exactly what it means, it's just too real for me to think about right now.

My brain backtracks. "Em, I'm fine. I'm totally fine. It's nothing to worry them about. Imagine what this news would do to Mom."

My sister's face falls even more, and the guilt kicks me in the gut. That was low, but I'm desperate. At least the part about it not being as bad as Emma's is true.

"How can you be fine? I don't believe you."

"Then I'll prove it!" I blurt out. "I *can* do the race. I can absolutely deliver your letter. It'll make the news. *Girl with Stargardt's helps raise awareness of the disease by having her sister deliver a letter by dog team.* You'll see. I'm totally fine."

Emma hesitates. A sudden shriek comes from the pen. The yearlings' play fight ends abruptly. "But then why did you just say you *couldn't* do it?"

"Well, you surprised me. But now that I'm thinking about it, yeah, I can. I just wanted you to know."

"Well, what can you see? Can you see Sumo?"

"Yes."

"Do you have the purple thing in the middle of your eyes? Can you see colors? What about me? Can you see my face?"

"Yes, I can see your squirrelly little face with the booger sticking out of your nose."

She laughs and wipes her nose with the back of her mitten. "So, you think you can do the mail run? Like, for real? You won't get hurt?" I can tell she's torn between worrying over my safety and wanting so badly for me to run the race.

"Yes, yes! I can do it! Imagine telling all your friends that their letters will be carried by your own dogs." I pause. "We don't have to say anything about this to anyone else, okay? We'll keep it between you and me."

The silence next is so heavy, the dogs pause to stare at us. For a beat, the kennel is ominously still. Waiting.

"Okaaay," Emma says. "But if your vision gets worse or it's too dangerous, you have to stop. You have to scratch the race, okay? And then you have to tell Mom and Dad. Or I will. Deal?" Emma still looks worried.

"Deal. If I don't deliver your letter, we tell them." I reach forward and take her hand. We shake on it.

"Here." Em digs into her pocket and pulls out her magnifier. She hands it to me. "Just in case you need help reading something, you should keep this. I've got my other one in my room."

"Thanks, but I don't need it." I wrap my fingers around Emma's magnifier. What I don't mention is that I know she has one in her room. I've borrowed it to do homework when no one was looking.

Nervous energy flows through me; I've avoided the disaster of Emma telling Mom and Dad. My legs jitter as we make our way up to the house, my sister gripping my arm. I adjust my sunglasses and angle the visor of my ball cap down in an effort to see where we're going on the well-tramped snowy trail.

After keeping this secret even from myself, I feel a weird mix of relief and regret that I've shared it with my sister. Of all the people to tell, Em understands the most. I press her hand with mine in a rush of emotion.

It isn't until later, when I'm setting the table, that what I've done really sinks in.

October 23, 1896

Dearest William,

You have been gone so long I have taken to reading the northern newspapers for lack of letters from you. Apparently a farmer's unfortunate pig had its ears chewed off by wolves. It has become quite famous, people traveling just to view the "earless pig." Why on earth do you wish to work in such a place? . . .

Anna has written a letter, which I have enclosed, along with a box of my butterscotch cookies that you so enjoy.

Your sister, Margaret

CHAPTER 4

One day before the race

The weeks after our secret deal were filled with race preparation. Measuring and stuffing frozen raw meat into bags, sewing booties, deciding which dogs would be in my race team, arguing over which batteries lasted longer in cold temperatures. A hundred and one chores needed doing.

Through it all, I worried that Emma would slip up and say something. She never did. Not once did she betray me. I felt the shift in our relationship. We were more a team than ever now that we had this thing looming that would define our future.

The mushers' meeting deadline felt a safe distance away. There was so much to do before the race, and I didn't have time to think about how I was going to actually race it. Until the day of the meeting arrived.

That morning we load the truck with the dogs, musher gear,

dog gear, sleds, quick-change runners, food, and a bucket of different brands of batteries. And then all four of us cram in for the forty-five-minute drive north to Sault Ste. Marie, Ontario. The meeting is at the Ermatinger House Museum, a national historic site that used to be a Hudson's Bay Company post. We also need to have all the dogs checked by the veterinarians, who are across the street at the plane museum's parking lot, where there is more room.

We arrive at the Ermatinger House slightly late, since one of us insisted on stopping along the way for a pee. Hazards of little sisters.

"We'll drop the dogs, McKenna," Dad says. "Get in there!"

I stumble inside and wait near the doorway. It takes a million years for my eyes to adjust from the light outside. People of all ages are packed around tables spread out through a room with a big stone fireplace and hand-hewn-log walls decorated with furs. Suddenly, I'm the one who has to pee.

Officials at the front of the room are showing a PowerPoint presentation. There's a lady who's already started her speech. I've missed the instructions on how to get to the McNabb staging area, where the race will begin tomorrow.

"And as a reminder, I wanted to briefly go over the required gear. It's listed on page two in your packets."

I search for an empty chair close to the front, but there aren't any. I have to sit near the back squeezed between a man and a woman who are both wearing what look like entire wolves on their heads.

"Where did you get your packet?" I ask the woman.

She points to the table right by the entrance. I'll have to get mine later.

"This is the same list you received in your e-mail," the announcer says. As she ticks off the items on the list, I peer around. I'm comforted to see that the table directly in front of me has a row of mushers about my age. At least, I assume they're mushers. They're dressed with various earflapped hats and anoraks and have the telltale odor of dog. Or it could be that they're just handlers — helpers for the actual musher running the race. My whole family will be my handlers, waiting for me at each leg. Dad took the week off, and Em got excused from school.

"In addition," the announcer says, "you will need to carry on your person a lighter, matches, a knife, and a survival blanket in case you get separated from your team. Officials may ask to see these items at any checkpoint."

Yes, yes. We packed all that and then some. I continue checking out the competition but can't make out details of people beyond my own table. Everyone is looking up at the screen at the front of the room. Everyone is looking with eyes that work.

In an instant, my mind goes to the place I've been avoiding. A tsunami of grief swells inside me. Grief over my fear for a future with low vision. I struggle to swallow the lump in my throat and shove my worries back down. This is not the time to deal with them.

"Next, we'll go over the race route," the announcer continues. "The Great Superior Mail Run is the first of its kind, celebrating the pioneer mail carriers who, a century ago, delivered mail and news of the world to the isolated communities along the shore of this great lake. So, for the most part, the trail follows the original route along the sections of lake ice that are travelable."

She puts up a map that I really wish I could see.

"We're mixing traditional stage-stop-race formats with a section of a long-distance-race format for a total of three hundred and fifty-four kilometers, making us a qualifier for the Yukon Quest."

Cheers break out from across the room as my insides tighten. That's over two hundred miles.

The announcer continues describing the route. All the distances are in kilometers, but living in Sault Ste. Marie, Michigan, so close to Canada, I've gotten used to converting the mileage in my head.

When she mentions the last leg of the race is one hundred and eighty-one kilometers, though, I have to stop and think. That's one hundred and twelve miles, which means at least ten hours on the trail. I knew this was going to be tough, but suddenly I worry. Mom's confidence in the dogs and me has given me a false sense of security. Even though I've been racing dogs since I could walk, that's a *lot* of miles to cover alone across unfamiliar terrain. It's even more than the Midnight Run, which was ninety miles. And I did that when I could see.

"Officials will be keeping track of your racing times at all checkpoints. The times for all three legs of your race will be added together," she continues. "And the musher with the best combined time wins."

She finally looks up from her notes to see hands raised. "Yes?"

"How are the ice conditions?"

"Most of the ice is over eighty-five centimeters thick, so there's plenty of it this year. But of course, that's not uniform everywhere. Please stay on the marked trail. There are some areas around islands where ice is thin."

Wonderful. I tend to see signs only if they're right beside me, which means I'm usually past them by the time I see them.

And while the ice on the trail will be nearly three feet thick, who knows how thin the ice might be if I stray off the trail?

"You might have noticed the windrows of ground ice in Whitefish Bay are over seven meters tall. But you won't run into them out on the marked route. For the most part, the ice crossings are clear of obstacles. The Cascades will be the most challenging section of trail. We'll keep you updated on trail conditions at each checkpoint."

Wait. Back up. What's the Cascades?

"Now for the interesting part," the announcer says. "The mail."

Applause from the crowd, and I join in.

Officials hand out old-fashioned canvas bags. Emma's class already mailed their letters with the special Great Superior Mail Run envelopes. They went to the sorting post office. All letters we're carrying had to be in the system and stopped at the post office here for us to pick up. Then we'll haul the bags with us to the White River post office, the end of the race, where they will be stamped and put back into the regular mail.

When I'm given my mailbag, the weight of it surprises me. It has metal grommets along the top and a metal clip cinching it closed. Mom arranged it so I have the envelopes from Emma's class. As far as she's concerned, the whole point of my racing is to get the media coverage for Stargardt disease.

One particular morning keeps replaying in my mind. Em had made a joke. Mom was standing in the kitchen about ten feet from her and smiling. And when Emma said, "Are you smiling? I can't tell if you're smiling," Mom had a complete meltdown. She didn't come out of her room for hours, and when she did, her eyes were puffy and red. She wants a cure for this disease probably more than any person alive.

"The mail in these bags," the announcer says, "is protected under federal law and so should be entrusted only to postal workers. Therefore, in order for you to carry this mail, you need to be sworn in and be designated as temporary letter carriers. So if I could get everyone to stand."

It takes a moment. Once the noise of scraping chairs dies down, the crowd grows serious, as though the mention of a ceremony makes everyone feel a bigger responsibility. Everyone here has to make a commitment. But no one has more riding on the task of delivering the mail than me.

"Now raise your right hand and repeat after me. 'I'—then state your name—'do solemnly swear to protect the mail entrusted to me,'" the lady says.

The rest of the room repeats her words. The rumbling of voices reverberates through my body. There's power in this, in standing here with my right hand raised and swearing to protect the mail that I have clutched in my left.

"'And return it to the official postal representative on Tuesday afternoon at the White River post office.'"

We all repeat the words. And with that, I'm an official mail carrier. Carrying a letter that I have to deliver or my whole world will change.

OCTOBER 23, 1896

DEAR UNCLE WILLIAM,

YOU WILL NEVER GUESS WHAT HAS HAPPENED SINCE YOU LEFT. I LOST A TOOTH. SORRY, IT HAS A BIT OF MUD INSIDE I COULD NOT GET OUT. CHARLIE STOMPED ON IT WITH HIS BIG HOOF, BUT IT DID NOT BREAK! SO I AM SENDING YOU MY LUCKY TOOTH TO HELP YOUR JOURNEY. WHEN YOU COME HOME YOU CAN TAKE ME TO SEE THE DIVING HORSE. IT JUMPS FROM A TOWER INTO THE TORONTO HARBOUR. PLEASE WRITE TO ME.

LOVE, ANNA

CHAPTER 5

Stage one: Sault Ste. Marie to Batchawana Bay checkpoint
38 miles

The person who invented mass starts should be strangled slowly. Obviously it was a non-musher who had the bright idea of making all the racers leave together. To begin, we have to lie on the ground next to our sleds, inside sleeping bags. Once the blare of the horn goes off—startling all the dogs—mushers have to spring out of their bags, jam their boots on, and start hooking up their teams. As if one screaming, frothing team of dogs at a time isn't enough, the entire yard of dogs is clipped onto ganglines, right next to one another. The noise level builds until the crazed panic in the air sticks to everyone.

Definitely a spectator sport. I don't know any musher who enjoys mass starts. So when I found out at the meeting that the race was going to have a mass start, I added it to the list of Reasons I Should Have Told Em No.

Now that the start is about to happen, I'm forced to admit I shouldn't be doing this race at all. Thankfully, the sky is overcast. There's a constant light without the variables of shadows, the kind of light my eyes like. So I can see pretty well.

But my other senses are assaulted.

The smell of the dogs' nervous diarrhea, pee-soaked straw, and bloody chicken water, along with the smell of ripe mushers, hangs all around me. On top of that, I can almost taste the promise of snow on its way. The icy feel coats the air, making balls of frost form on the hair that sticks out from under my hat.

The mob of huskies creates a cacophony of noise — barking, howling, crying, yipping, growling. Mushers are yelling at their dogs, yelling to one another; spectators are laughing and shrieking. And above it all, I can actually tell each of my own dogs' voices apart by the pitch of their frantic screaming. They're telling me the reasons they need to go. Right *now*.

I agree. Let's get out of here.

"Ten minutes to start," Mom says. She's holding Emma's hand. Poor Em. Mom's doing this in front of all the kids in Emma's class, who were bused here to watch the start of the race, and half the city. And to add to our embarrassment, we're parked right next to an enormous statue of anatomically correct cows. The female cow is sitting on the shoulders of the bull and her udders are hanging on either side of his head. It is very weird and tall and I try to ignore it and hope nobody is taking pictures of me with those horrifying pink udders in the background.

I check again to make sure I'm ready. Every dog is harnessed. The gangline is carefully laid out so all I have to do is bring the dogs up and clip them in. All the lines are in the right place, set to go.

I pull on my race bib over my anorak, sit on my sleeping bag, kick off my boots, and command my fingers to stop shaking. My leaders, Mustard and Twix, are closest to me on the dropline attached to the dog truck. Mustard burbles a long, involved story. He's always been a talker. Twix just whines softly.

My two swing dogs, Lizard and Damage, are next. Damage is screaming as if someone is ripping off his toenails. *Aeeeiiiya, aeeei-iya, aeeiiya.*

Lizard is mumbling to himself underneath the truck. He hates crowds and always hides at events.

In team position are Saga and Aspen. Strange to have two females running together, but they're buds. Except at hookup, when I have to watch they don't rip each other's faces off. I can hear them gearing up to do just that.

"Saga! That's not nice!"

Last are my wheel dogs, Haze and Sumo. Haze has a polite

little howl, as if she's saying, *Excuse me, I think we should be running now.*

And Sumo, sweet Sumo. Em's dog. I shouldn't have brought this dog. Sumo is a B-string dog. Actually, no. Not even second choice for a race team. He's too big, for one thing, prime for over-heating. He's sixty-four pounds. No other dog on the team is over fifty-five. And he's far too powerful. The fact that he's here just proves how completely nuts I am. If we get in trouble, guaranteed he's going to be involved somehow.

"Sumo is excited," Emma says. Her eyes shine; she's vibrating worse than I am.

"He's a star," I say.

Sumo was Em's only choice for my team. She can't run the race, but her dog can. I didn't have the heart not to bring him. My only hope is that he burns out on the first leg and I get to drop him at the Batchawana checkpoint.

Suddenly, the countdown. "Ten, nine, eight . . ."

Get your head in the game. This is happening. Heart thumping, I climb into the sleeping bag and lie down. A few flakes begin to fall and melt on my face.

". . . three, two, one, *go!*"

The sound of the horn rips through my brain. I leap up. Get tangled in the lining. Tumble onto the snow with my legs all twisted up. I crawl out, pull on my boots, shove the bag into my sled, and then turn to the dogs.

And trip on my own sled runner. I fall flat.

"Get up, McKenna!" Em says helpfully.

By the time I've picked myself up, I see the musher next to me has half his team hooked. *How the*—

No one can help me. Mushers have to hook up their own teams. Dad watches while pacing the length of the truck. I grab Mustard and scuttle with him to the front of the gangline. I see the musher on the other side of me leading two dogs at once. That's the trouble with my eyesight lately—I can see what's to the side of me better than what's straight ahead.

Focus.

I peer at the tugline snap and clip it on the first try. Then I race toward Twix, who's got both front feet out reaching for me as far as her line allows. As I'm bringing her, hopping on her back legs, a team comes out of nowhere and runs over my gangline. The musher's got both feet on his brake, so the points grab my line and drag poor Mustard backwards.

"Your brake!" I screech. "Lift your brake!"

Then he's gone. So much for my gangline being neatly laid out.

Mustard doesn't even bat an eye, but now I'm shaking so badly, I can barely clip in Twix. *Come on, you're okay,* I tell myself.

The urgency in the air is making my fingers fumble. Somehow I get the team hooked up. The line is all over the place, but I've done this a million times. Finally, everyone is set. I pull the snub. "Ready? All right!"

We're off, flying across the parking lot. Except there are many teams around me also flying across the parking lot. It occurs to me that we're all going to bottleneck at the one narrow opening of the trailhead. We're not all going to fit. Epic collision in three, two, one . . .

I jam on the brake, but since there's not much snow cover, that hardly slows us down. Plus — Sumo.

A sled narrowly misses colliding with us, but we inch ahead. It's actually a good thing I can't see details. I just trust my leaders. They navigate the mess of teams around us, and suddenly, we're on the trail.

Away.

Monday, January 28, 2019

Dear McKenna,

Weird sending a letter, right? But you hardly text anymore. I figured this would get your attention through your
dogs! I had to buy one of these race envelopes, so I hope
you're happy. Ha! I miss you, you know? It was so boring
at cross-country practice. I had to run with Hannah. But
that helped me build my speed trying to get away from
her talking about herself.

I'm not sure what I've done, but I think you're mad at me
about something.

Still your best friend,
Gabs

36

CHAPTER 6

Batchawana Bay, late afternoon

After our encounter with the blind lead dog and the other mushers out on the lake, the team and I are happy to have the trail to ourselves.

I keep thinking we'll run into the girl again, but we don't overtake anyone.

The dogs are pumped, just steaming along. I only wish the clouds would cover the sun like they did when we started this morning. The blue sky is streaked with wispy clouds and the sunlight is bouncing off every surface around me. I can hardly see where we're going. It's like driving a speeding train with the front window covered in soot. It makes me think of all the amazing things in my life that I'll miss being able to see clearly, and the sadness flares again.

But I can see the shoreline as we go by. When the lake was

freezing, the wind created weird sculptures out of the waves. Clear blue ice has been rolled into little caves with smooth boulders and bridges in one bay, while in another bay, facing in a slightly different direction, the wind has formed sharp shark teeth of ice. Windswept pines daring to grow near the shore are encased in thick white ice from the freezing spray. They look like hunched, spooky snowmen.

Mustard and Twix follow the trail off the lake and through a stand of spruce. After a while, I relax. This is like being out on a training run. I love being out on training runs. We're totally good.

I've been out alone on runs a lot lately. It's my only solace after school, where pretending nothing's wrong has become more and more stressful. I think back to last year when my best friend, Gabby, used to come with me, ride in the sled, ready to jump out and help whenever needed. But this season, I noticed I couldn't see things the way I used to. On the trail, I knew where the turns were, but I couldn't tell how soon they'd come up. It was disorienting. I started crashing.

And in school, I couldn't read the board. Even though it didn't happen suddenly, it felt like it had. The words and numbers kept getting smaller and blurrier week by week. And one day, I just couldn't see anything on it. I started to sneak in after everyone left the class so I could stand right next to the board to read it. I've had to make a rule: Never read in front of anyone.

This past semester, Mom and Dad put my sliding grades down to my worry over Em. In some ways, it was nice to know I could hide in plain sight around them while they were so focused on the one major problem that all of us shared—my sister's low vision.

But in truth, school had become harder in more ways than just my grades. For instance, a girl I hardly know, Jessica, has the same long blond hair as Gabby. She has the same body shape; she even has the same pink backpack. I was constantly embarrassing myself by calling out to her, mistaking her for Gabs. I couldn't recognize my best friend anymore. Couldn't recognize any of my friends unless they were close. They'd get mad at me for ignoring them. People in the halls would wave, and I'd wave back, only to realize they were greeting the person behind me. How mortifying is that? But the frightening part was *why*.

Now that I'm sure I've got Stargardt disease, I'm even more determined to keep it from Mom. If she knew, she'd force me to get tested. And as soon as I got diagnosed, she'd start treating me the way she treats my sister. And she treats Em like she's helpless.

Up till now, no one has worried about me, even with Em having it, because at our annual ophthalmologist visits, my eyes have always been clear. Even last year, when the doctor examined my eyes, he said they didn't have the little white flecks at the backs of the retinas.

If I don't get tested, and no one knows, then everything can stay the same. And since there's no treatment, nothing can be done about it anyway.

But hiding it meant more time spent alone. Being too busy to eat lunch with people. Missing the afterschool events committee—I couldn't help make decorations with those tiny cutouts. Friday nights I couldn't go to Chloe's with everyone to watch movies. I blew Gabby off running dogs. I made up excuses why she couldn't come one day. And the next. And pretty soon, she stopped asking me to do anything with her.

Everyone stopped asking.

An electric jolt goes through me as my team disappears around a corner. I slam the brake. It's the worst thing to do and far too late. The sled lurches over a hill. It careens down the slope. We jerk to the left. Teeter on the right runner. I slam my weight to the other runner, but it's not enough. The sled crashes onto its side. I'm left skidding after it on my belly.

"Whoa! Whoa, Mustard. Stop!"

My team flies down the trail as if nothing happened. Every rut jars my body. Every snowball smashes in my face. *Ow!* And that was a chunk of ice.

I cling to the runner with a clawlike grip. Desperately, I pull myself closer to the sled. The brake won't work when the sled is sideways. I don't even bother with it. But the rubber drag reaches to the ground. I grab hold. Press down. Try to control the team. There's no slowing their crazy charge.

Snow flies off my boots, off my elbows. The sideways runner bites into the hard trail, and a rooster tail of spray follows us. I've got it in my mouth, up my nose. I pull myself hand over hand, climbing partly upright to reach for the snow hook in its cradle.

I'm yelling at the dogs to slow down. Of course they think I mean "go faster." There's nothing more exciting than a good clean run down a trail with your musher screaming in terror behind you. They live for this.

I finally knock the snow hook down. It bounces close to my face, nearly relocating my front teeth. I grab a prong and manage to dig the points into the trail. They gouge out two long grooves as the team slows down. We finally stop.

I pick myself up. The dogs are looking back at me in surprise. *What's the matter?* they seem to ask.

"Never mind me. I'm fine, thanks."

I take stock of the damage. My anorak is stiff and cold. I fluff it out to dump the snow. I've got some impressive road rash up my right arm from my wrist to my elbow. That's cool. But then

I notice something not cool. I madly clutch at my chest and neck. I've lost my sunglasses.

"Oh no!" I squint against the glare and spin around, hoping they're hanging off me by a strap somewhere. No.

"No!" The blinding whiteness of the snow pierces my eyes without the protection of my dark shades. Plus, I have to protect my maculas. The last thing I want is for my vision to get worse. The number-one most important piece of equipment I have, and I've already lost it. The first day isn't even over yet.

Why didn't I bring two pairs?

I glance behind and see something dark on the trail. Are those my shades? I hesitate, not wanting to leave my team. That's a rookie move. And it was almost a disaster back at the lake.

But I desperately need those glasses. I sprint toward the dark object. I'm almost on top of it before I see that it's just a piece of driftwood or something frozen into the trail. I pivot and race back to my dogs. I'm frazzled by the time I grab the sled.

"Gotcha," I say with relief.

Arooooooo, Mustard replies.

That makes Damage start up again. *Aeeeiiiya, aeeeiiya, aeeiiya.*

And now the whole team is lunging and screaming to go. Enough resting. More *running.* It's too early in the race for them to want to stop for long. Sumo alone is going to rip out that snow hook any minute.

I'll have to find another pair of shades when we get to the checkpoint. Until then, I'll just pull my hat lower. Hurriedly, I jump back onto the runners and take a deep breath.

My awesome dogs are leaping in the air, ready for another adventure. The sled is vibrating under me; the power of my speeding train seeps into my blood. I bend and yank the hook, and we blast off.

Who needs a clear windshield anyway?

January 16, 2019

Dear Nana,

We're writing letters to be sent by sled dogs! Emma is
a girl in my class and she has a dog team. But Emma
doesn't run since she's blind and she can't do anything.
She can't even butter her toest in food class. The
teacher told her to try. I helped her becase I didn't want
her to get in trouble. She's nice.

Love, Phoebe
PS when we come this summer, can we go horsback riding
again? That was fun!

CHAPTER 7

Batchawana Bay checkpoint

I'm resting with my dogs when the boy and his team come through.

I don't recognize him from this distance, but then I hear his voice. His is the first team to arrive since I got here, so I assume the volunteers told him what they told me about this nice spot behind the Obadjiwan Conference Center.

We're blocked from the wind. It whistles across the lake ice, picking up fine particles of snow like grains of sand. Spindrift, pointy and sharp, gets into everything. It's a relief to be out of its reach and tucked out of the way of the teams coming through.

I wanted quiet for the dogs so they could have uninterrupted rest while we wait for my family with the dog truck. The plan was for us to meet here this afternoon, but my team and I got here faster than anyone thought we would, in just three and a half hours.

Sumo gets up to rearrange his straw to his liking. He paws at it, nosing it this way and that. With a loud sigh, he lies back down. Dramatic.

I take the hint, roll off my sled, and give Sumo another flake of straw. "For a big tough guy, you're really not that tough, diva." I run my fingers through his surprisingly soft cheek fur.

The boy's voice gets louder as he steers his team my way. "Go on, Zest. Haw, haw, haw, haw." He gives quick, staccato commands to his leaders. His dogs snake their way toward me.

Mustard lifts his head and gives a soft *woooo*, but most of my dogs don't even twitch. All of them are curled up in their matching blue fleece jackets with wind-stopper shells. Saga has her head draped over Aspen so that their necks are intertwined. They know well the rhythm of racing. Run. Rest. Run. Rest. And they're just as serious about their rest as they are about the running.

"Oh, hello again. Mind if we crash here? Looks like my handlers and dog truck haven't arrived yet." The boy tosses a bale of straw that he must've grabbed when he signed in at the checkpoint off the front of his sled.

"I'm Guy, by the way." He pronounces his name like *geek* without the *k*—the French way.

"Doesn't that confuse your dogs?" I say. "Having your name rhyme with *gee*?" I overemphasize the soft *g*.

"Nah, they're bilingual." Guy stomps on his snow hook and then moves up his team unclipping tuglines. "Plus I only talk about myself in the third person when they aren't around."

I watch as he spreads the straw among his dogs. His Euro-hound sniffs at it suspiciously. The sleek floppy-eared dog is wearing neon-green leg wraps.

"They've got hot water inside," I say, noticing his dog cooler.

"Oh, great. Thanks. And now Guy is wondering if you're going to share your name or if he's going to have to guess from the list of female mushers in the race."

"Your dogs are listening," I remind him.

"Touché," he says. "That's French too, by the way."

We look at each other for a beat. "You aren't really French, are you?"

"What?" He draws himself up, then gives in. "Well, I tried to learn, but it's hard. My dad should've talked French to me more when I was a baby with a moldable brain. Guy's brain is old now." He grins at me before kneeling in front of his wheel dogs.

The coal-colored one immediately rolls over on her back, her bootied feet pointing in the air. Guy rubs her belly as he removes the booties. He coos, "Who's my cuddle pumpkin? Oh, you like that, don't you, Groot?"

He peels off his hat and leans in to rub his head across her neck, the whole time murmuring in something like baby talk. Guy allows Groot to wrap her front paws around his ears and nibble at his hair.

"Cuddle pumpkin?" I ask.

"She likes it. Don't judge."

"Not judging," I say. Any boy who can act like a goofball with his dogs in front of other people is okay in my book. In fact, it's sort of the ultimate test of character. "But actually, totally judging the name Groot. So unoriginal."

"Her litter was born during my movie phase. She's running with her brother Yoda." He points to the nearly identical wheel dog beside her. "And that's another brother of hers, Captain Jack. I might still be in my movie phase, sadly. I feel a Mantis coming on."

"No!" I laugh. "Well, it's better than Star Lord. Good bit of self-control there."

I reach into my sled bag and find the stash of dinners that Mom prepared and froze in Ziplocs. I can't tell what this one is, but boil-in-bag surprise is my favorite. The meals are exactly where they're supposed to be, midway up my bag on the left side.

If there's one thing I've learned watching Emma live with this condition for the past two years, it's that organization is key.

I turn to leave Guy to his chores. But as I head inside, I remember his question.

"McKenna Barney," I call to him. No idea why I feel the need to say my full name. Am I trying to intimidate him? Maybe he's never heard of my mom.

He's chopping bits of meat into his cooler. He stops to cover his heart with his hand, but he's holding the ax and nearly loses his nose.

"Nice tactic, Barney," he yells. "Distract me when I'm armed and dangerous. You trying to cut your competition down? I'm onto you."

I surely hope he's not.

Dear Ant Diane

We have to rite letters in our class to someone. Mom
said I shud pick you because you love getting letters. Why
woudn't you want to facetime with me instead? Then I
can show you my lose tooth. Letters are dum.

Love Jake

CHAPTER 8

I've eaten and I'm back out with the dogs when my family arrives.

"McKenna!" Mom screeches out the window of the truck.

I can't see her across the parking lot full of dog trucks and mushers and handlers. Now everyone knows my name. Not helpful when trying to act normal and avoid anyone watching me too much, but I'm happy to hear her. They drive up and park next to us.

"Sorry, we got held up trying to find straw," Dad says, clapping me on the back. We weren't allowed to bring it across the border. "You made good time?"

"Yeah, we had a great run," I say, ducking my head to untangle Lizard. He's excited to see the dog truck. He knows there's warm soup coming next. But he's not that crazy about all the strange people around.

"They're looking good, McKenna." A vet has come to check the dogs. She's kneeling in the straw inspecting Mustard's feet.

Mustard doesn't appear at all concerned that the vet is spreading his toes apart, pinching his skin over his shoulder blades, and pulling the skin down under his eyes to shine her flashlight into them. Mustard solemnly stares back at her, and my heart squeezes with as much pride as if I'd birthed him myself.

"Any worries?" she asks.

"Aspen has been pacing a bit. That little brown dog on the end. I just massaged her front shoulder. She injured it last year, but she's been pulling steady." I bend to hold Aspen's head while the vet manipulates her joints.

Mom puts out a camp chair for Em. "How are you, honey?"

"I'm fine," Emma says.

Mom helps her to the chair and then heads toward the center with a load of gear.

"Hey, squirt," I say. "Did you have a fun day off school?"

"We went sightseeing," she says, and then she grins, pointing to her eyes in her typical self-deprecating way. "I'm really good at it."

Dad rummages through the bowls in the back of the truck. He has all the dogs' attention. I'm relieved to be with my family again, but I'm also nervous.

My parents are used to living with Em. They know the signs of Stargardt's. They'll notice something is off with me if I let my guard down for an instant. I have to force myself not to angle my head to look at things the way Emma does. It's exhausting and stressful, and it's the reason I've avoided being around them. But here at the checkpoints, I'm forced into it. More than anything, I want to keep them from asking questions.

"Clean bill of health," the vet says. "Keep up the good work." She moves on to the next team.

I breathe a sigh. As long as my dogs are healthy and strong, we might get through this race.

"Where's Sumo?" Emma asks.

I bring Sumo over to the truck and clip him to a drop chain. Emma squeaks and kneels next to him and wraps her arms around his neck. I'm worried she's going to say something about my vision, not realizing Dad is in earshot.

"No reporters here yet," I say to distract her. "But once I start dazzling everyone with my times, I'm sure they'll be at the next checkpoint. I've been practicing what I'm going to say about carrying your letter."

"Obviously *I'll* be doing the interviews. Duh," Emma says. "I'm the cute blind kid. You're just the musher. And past the age of cuteness. If they interview me, I'll get maximum coverage. Magazines, TV, YouTube. It'll go viral."

The floodlights in the parking lot come on above us. They cast half her face in shadow, but I can hear the teasing in her voice. She knows I'm worried about her telling, and she's letting me know she won't. But we're going to have to talk later in private so I can assure her I'm okay. As long as I don't let myself dwell too much on losing my vision, I will be okay.

I poke her belly. She reaches out to take a swipe at me. Then Mom appears around the corner.

"I've put your stuff inside—oh, Emma, don't sit so close to Sumo while he's on the drop chain. McKenna, what are you thinking? She can't see the chain. She could get whacked in the face."

"For God's sake, Beth. She's fine," Dad says. "You can see the chain, right, Emma?"

"Sorry," I say immediately so Emma doesn't have to answer.

This has been Dad's favorite kind of question since the big moment we got the results of the genetic tests and learned that Emma got Stargardt's because she inherited recessive genes for it from both parents. Each of them took this news differently. Dad refused to accept it. And Mom has turned into a person obsessed, as though she can shelter Emma with the strength of her guilt. At least that was the end of the argument over whose fault it was.

Mom whisks Emma to a safer location.

Dad finishes what he's doing with the gear in the back of the truck and comes over. He hands me the poop scooper. "Watch behind you there. Twix made a mess."

"Yeah, I know. I was getting to it." Even though I can't see it in the glare of the floodlights, I still have a nose.

Soon, I hear Mom's hurried boots crunching toward us again.

"I got Emma set up in a corner of the dining hall. I'll feed her now," she says to Dad.

"Let her do it! Don't forget what the food-tech teacher said."

"Just leave it alone, okay?"

I can feel the tense vibes and busy myself, pretending not to hear. Mom climbs into the back seat of the truck and pulls out Emma's bag. I notice she leaves Em's cane that I was careful to bring along.

Before running back inside, she pats my shoulder. "Thank God you're whole, McKenna, and we don't have to worry about you."

I feel as though I've been doused in ice water. "You don't have to worry about me, Mom."

My parents start walking toward the center. I hear their angry whispers receding as they leave me to finish the chores. That suits me. Now I don't have to stress about things like banging my head on the doors of the dog boxes.

After I've scooped, I tear apart the inside of our truck looking for a spare pair of sunglasses. Nothing. My anxiety levels hitch up a notch as I imagine going out on the trail again without them. I'll have to ask my parents if they have any.

I jump out of the truck and then pause a moment to listen to everything going on around me. The shifting of the lake ice. The popcorn sound of snow pellets hitting the ground. The noise of teams still coming in, dogs arguing at the next dog truck, people laughing and calling to one another across the parking lot. I stand alone in the middle of it all, thinking about Mom's words.

I'm *whole?* Does that mean that Emma *isn't* whole? And what would I be with Stargardt disease?

December 13, 1896

Dear Margaret,

We have reached humanity! After six days, we arrived in the port of Sault Sainte Marie with much commotion and celebration. "The posties are here!" men were crying out to one another, their laughter ringing through the town as we made our way up Queen Street on frozen limbs.

The smell of smoke coming from the fires had me as joyful as the men running toward us like a stampede of buffalo . . .

Your loving brother, William

CHAPTER 9

The laughter from the campfire draws me over.

I'm not ready to sleep. Nervous energy still courses through me. I'd left my family in the computer room and wandered over to check on the dogs, but they didn't appreciate being disturbed.

All the other mushers have their chores done too. Because this is the stage-stop part of the race, they've timed today's leg and we don't run again until tomorrow. Now the dogs have been fed, watered, massaged, all tended to and tucked in their beds. We have time to relax before the next leg of the race tomorrow.

I stumble over the brush bow of a sled parked nearby, and the people talking pause in their conversation. Has everyone turned to look at me? This was a mistake. What was I thinking, coming over here? I wave and try to act natural as I search for a seat.

A hand grabs my arm and pulls me onto a bench. "Sit before you fall down. Sheesh, you're really tired, huh?" It's Guy.

"Sorry, long day." I glance around and see several more mushers our age.

The fire licks the sky, sending out sparks. I feel the blast of heat on my face and stick out my fingers. Man, that feels good.

"Did you see the moose?" a girl asks. She's sitting close to Guy. Like, tragically close. So obvious.

"*Did* I?" says a large kid next to me. He has a high voice that doesn't match the space he seems to take up. "That moose nearly plowed through my team."

"As if, Harvey," Guy says with a laugh. "You forget I was right behind you."

"Well, it seemed like the moose was about to turn any minute. You never know what those swamp donkeys are going to do. Tiny brains." Harvey taps his forehead for emphasis.

It's nice to be around other mushers, especially ones my age. I have a lot of friends at school, and they think it's cool that I run dogs and sometimes even win races. But they can't understand what it's like to be a musher. Everyone here knows. They love their dogs as much as I do. We all *get it*. All the hours of training, being out in blizzards, in sleet, in the dark, feeding, doing chores, worrying over injury, bursting with pride when a yearling does well. I don't have to try and explain how the joy of running dogs seeps into you and attaches to your soul.

All around me, I can hear different conversations and I realize some of them know one another or have raced together before.

"You running Beaver in lead? I'd never guess she'd have a head for it."

"What are you feeding for snacks? Mine seem to be going off lamb."

"I'd put Saran around his wrist first, before the wrap. Keeps the ligaments warm."

I listen and enjoy the feeling of being with everyone. Something unfurls inside me. I *had* friends. But it's been a while since I've let myself be part of a group.

My attention snaps to a conversation when I hear the word *Cascades*.

"It's supposed to be bad this year because of all the freezing and thawing we've had," someone says. I can't see who's talking; she's a few seats away from me.

"What's the Cascades?" I ask.

"It's the name for the section of trail over the mountain," a male voice says. "Instead of switchbacks, it's just one long death spiral down. The trouble is the water runoff from the cliffs. It freezes, and the buildup of ice makes the trail like a luge. So you gotta run across where the ice forms. And the trail isn't flat, it's sloped, like this."

I assume he's holding his hands up to show a disastrous angle.

Harvey takes up the story. "So if you start to slide, you're *cascading* your butt all the way down." Since he's beside me, I can see his hands diving down and then blowing up as he demonstrates a crash, complete with sound effects.

I try to ignore the growing horror of my situation, but it's insistent. How am I going to get through that? It's all my worst fears come to life: I could get the dogs hurt. They could slip, sprain, or injure joints. I'd have no control. And it sounds like we could all plummet right off the mountain.

The main thing I'm concerned about is the dogs. Keeping them safe. So, really, I should just stand up right now, march over to the officials, and scratch.

But I don't. I stare into the flames, trying to figure out what I'm going to do. I've got a bag of mail here that I've sworn to protect. But more important, if I don't deliver Em's letter, she's going to tell. I'm more committed to this than anything I've ever done.

Tomorrow should be an easy run across Pancake Bay and then through some old logging roads. I can do tomorrow. For now, I decide to be like one of my dogs and just live in the moment.

December 14, 1896

Dear Margaret,

I must describe again our arrival for it has etched itself in my mind. Tears were streaking down the men's faces as they read letters from their loved ones. I can now conceive why mail couriers like Mr. Miron continue this job after the struggles that we've faced. For the souls in these remote communities, we are their only contact with the outside world throughout the long cold winter . . .

I only wish that I had a letter from you.

Your loving brother, William

CHAPTER 10

G uy nudges me.

As the fire pops and sparks beside us, he pulls a book from his pocket. "The best part of this race is the fact that we're going over the same trails that the couriers ran." He thrusts the book at me. "Look at this! These are collections of actual letters William Desjardins wrote when he traveled through here."

Without thinking, I bring my head closer and peer at it so I can see what he's holding. Then my heart leaps. I jerk my head up in a panic. Rule number one: Never read in front of people! It's not as if I can pull out Em's magnifier right now either.

"Um. It's late. I'd better get some sleep." I stand to leave.

Guy grabs my hand and pulls me back down to the bench. The touch of his skin on mine shocks me into silence. I notice how warm his hand is and then it's gone.

"I haven't told you the best part. William *Desjardins*—he's actually my relative. My great-great-grandfather!" Guy's so enthusiastic, he doesn't seem to notice that he held my hand. "He needed to get to White River, and the fastest way at the time was with the dog couriers running this mail route."

He begins to read out loud from his book of letters. Without him looking at me, I have time to gather my thoughts. I can watch him from the corner of my eye and listen to the sound of his voice. It has a nice tone. There's a good energy buzzing off him. He captures my full attention. The girl next to Guy gives up and wanders away.

When Guy finally pauses and looks up from his book, I'm torn from the spell he's cast. "Where did you find that? How do you know you're related?" I ask.

"I've been hearing about him my whole life. My grandpa Desjardins told me stories when I was young about his granddad's time with the couriers. And a while ago, he had this book made. It's the whole reason I wanted to run the race. In school, I even heard about Raymond Miron, the courier from Sault Ste. Marie who ran the mail with his dogs from Killarney to these very trails. And he got the same greeting every time he delivered the mail. His arrival at a community was an *event*. It almost makes you wish that texting wasn't invented. It would be so cool to bring the mail to people when it was really important. You know?"

I nearly tell him that some of us *are* carrying really important mail. It finally dawns on me. "That's why you're dressed as . . . what, a mail courier, right? 'Cause you're carrying the mail?"

Guy straightens the button things on his shoulders. "I know women can't resist a man in uniform, but I've got other priorities, ma'am. I have to get the mail through. At all costs, the mail must get through."

"You might be the weirdest person I've ever met."

"Come, now," he says. "I shall endeavor to be not weird."

I smile and shake my head. "So you're from here? You ever run the UP? The Upper Peninsula race in Michigan?"

"I did the Beargrease mid-distance last year."

"Cool! I ran the rec class when I was twelve. My mom ran behind me with her team."

"She running this one too?"

I hesitate. "No. Mom used to race. She did it for years before meeting my dad. You might recognize her name. Beth Barney?"

Guy shrugs.

"She was Beth Lee a long time ago when she won races. Now

she just stays home. She's made looking after my sister a full-time job."

"Why?"

I should *not* have brought this up. Best to stay away from the topic entirely. I should have led with my dad's business — pumping septic systems and renting out porta-potties. That always ends the conversation. But something about Guy keeps me talking. "Well, my mom's really protective of her."

"What's wrong with her?"

"Em's got some eyesight challenges. She could use vision-enhancing equipment, but my parents would rather fight about what she needs."

"Really? Is it progressive retinal atrophy?" Guy leans forward. "That's what Zesty has."

"No. She's got Stargardt disease. It's also called juvenile macular degeneration. It causes damage to the macula and nothing can be done about it."

"Oh, that sucks," Guy says. "There's no cure for Zesty either. But she doesn't seem to mind." Guy looks thoughtful for a moment. "Vision-enhancing equipment like what?"

"The school bought her this thing called CCTV. It's a TV screen at her desk that she uses to zoom in on the whiteboard so she can see it from where she's sitting. It enlarges words up to sixty times." I immediately think of my own troubles seeing the board. And I refuse to move closer to the front, since moving would look too suspicious.

"Why can't she just wear glasses?"

"If there's something wrong with your cornea—that's the camera lens in the front part of your eye—it can be fixed with glasses or surgery. Stargardt's affects the retina, which is at the back of your eye. Corrective glasses don't help. But she can be like any normal person if she uses her aids. And other equipment like voice technology, monoculars, large-print books, magnifiers, her cane." The more I talk about this, the more agitated I feel. "Hey, it's getting late. I'm going to get some sleep. Big day tomorrow beating you."

"Ha!" Guy jabs at the fire, and sparks illuminate the angles of his grin. They also illuminate his serious hat head. "You'll need a lot more than rest to beat me again. I'm onto you for real now."

As I stumble away from the fire, I feel that grin follow me. I normally don't like being watched, but this time, I don't mind at all.

Wednesday, January 16, 2019

Dear Foundation for Fighting Blindness,

My name is Emma and I have Stargardt disease. My sister,
McKenna, is bringing this letter with our dog team. I like
sitting in the sled with her when the dogs run. They love
it and they run FAST! Anyway, please, please find a cure
for Stargardt's. You have to help people see good again.
I don't like my mom being sad all the time. And I don't like
my dad being mad.

From Emma Barney

CHAPTER 11

Stage two: Batchawana Bay to Gargantua Harbour
78 miles

I hear someone's alarm going off.

What time is it? I jump up and then fall flat. *What's wrong with my feet?* I reach down and feel that my bootlaces are tied together. On purpose. Someone tied them in a knot. Did I fall asleep with my boots on? I was so tired last night, I stumbled into the computer room, found my bedroll laid out on the floor where I'd left it, and passed out.

I look around, trying to figure out what's going on. My watch reads 5:32 a.m. It's dark outside but there's light coming from the main dining room illuminating the sleeping forms over the floor. Some people are up, banging in the kitchen.

Dad appears beside me. Sees that I'm awake. Whispers, "Good, I was coming to make sure you're on schedule for feeding."

I nod and untie my laces. I have a sneaking suspicion who would prank me and I can't help grinning. Oh, he's going down.

It's that predawn pure black outside with a light east wind. The skin on my face tightens in the chill. *Crunch. Crunch.* The darkness makes my steps sound louder. Dog eyes shine back in the beam of my headlamp. They rise, shake; their collars jangle. On my knees, I make my way down the line, breathe in their morning dog smells. They blink sleep away.

Lizard uncurls and gives one of his trademark smiles, peeling his lips back in a toothy grin. Terrifying. Despite the crisp air, warmth spools off his soft parts like he's a cat who's been sleeping in the sun. On to Haze next. Noses touch. A whiskered sniff. I rub my fingers in her ears, which fold over at the tops. They're warm inside too. She goes still and closes her eyes.

The dogs stretch and wag, ready for the day. Sumo flaunts his tongue in a yawn. Damage pokes his nose too close to Aspen and then wisely retreats. Mustard has a lot to say, as usual, until Twix solemnly taps her front toes on his face.

Tap. Tap. Tap. Tap. Translation: *Will. You. Shut. It.*

I cook them a warm breakfast, then scoop poop. Mushers have to do all their own chores looking after their dogs. I'm glad for that; it makes a race better when you protect that bond between a musher and team. After chores, I go inside to eat a bowl of oatmeal with Em while the sky slowly brightens.

"Oh, good," Mom says when she sees me. "Help Emma eat while I pack up."

This is a heated point of contention in our household. Emma's counselor shared her food-tech teacher's concerns about Em not being able to spread butter on a piece of bread. She couldn't fill a glass of water from the tap. And she wouldn't eat food that she couldn't pick up with her fingers. I'm not sure why that was a shock to everyone, since this has been going on for years. The counselor basically blamed it on Mom, which started the angry discussions between our parents after we'd gone to bed.

I push the oatmeal toward Emma and clank the spoon against the bowl.

"Did you know you're in third place?" she says.

"Fifth place. The dogs were fast yesterday and the trails were no problem. Told ya." I'm careful what I say with Mom bustling nearby.

Em flashes me a secret smile but with a question clearly in it. She wants to know how my eyes are. At times like this, I really wish she could see my face. I squeeze her hand, and after a weighted pause, she nods. A full conversation in a few gestures.

I think back to all our conversations together, late at night on Emma's bed. I'd ask her over and over, "But what can you see?" It was so confusing because Emma couldn't explain it well. Sometimes she'd say she couldn't see the dogs in the dog yard, but other times she could. She couldn't see my face, but she saw a bat flitting over our heads. It was frustrating.

But now I understand. Everything depends on how much light there is, on the contrasts and the shadows. I can see things like the trees but not the details of the branches. Sometimes my brain plays tricks and I see things in the branches that aren't even there.

I look at Em now and I'm torn between fear that I'll be like her soon and guilt for thinking that way.

"So, you have to wait longer to go out, right?" Emma asks. "Since you're one of the faster teams?"

"Yeah, the mass start was just for the first day." I give a little cheer, waving my fist in the air. "From now on we'll go out in the opposite order of our times the day before. So I'll be fifth to last."

I shove a spoon of oatmeal in my mouth and stick my tongue out. Emma's expression doesn't change and I chide myself for trying. I swallow the sticky mess around the sudden lump in my throat. "It's going to take a little time getting the mail stamped at the post office this morning," I continue. "Then we start the race from there, so I should see you at the Gargantua checkpoint after dinner." I put extra enthusiasm in my voice to convince myself I'll get there.

"You okay, Emma?" Mom asks. She's got a load of gear in her arms, but she bends down to look at my sister's face.

"I'm fine, Mom."

I notice Mom carrying Emma's cane. I brought it inside so Emma could use it. It's the same white cane that the counselor from the Blind Institute gave Em at that first meeting two years ago. Emma needs to learn to use it, she'd said. Mobility training was part of what she'd need to be independent and look after herself. My parents looked physically ill seeing Emma with it in her hand, as if the cane made it real that there was something wrong with her. Hating the cane is the one thing they agree on.

I cram in the last spoonful of breakfast, jump up, and begin to layer on my gear for the day. Mom shifts a sleeping bag to one hand so she can wipe the side of Emma's mouth. It's okay that she doesn't wish me luck. She's busy with Em.

I hurry outside to prepare the sled and harness the dogs. It's an overcast morning. Perfect. But not as cold as I'd hoped. The dogs run faster on hard-packed frozen trails from cold nights.

"We'll have to make sure you don't get overheated today, right, chum?" I say to Sumo after pulling his harness over his wide head. He butts me with it. I don't see it in time and get my nose smashed.

"Ow! Meathead! I know you want to get going again." I give him a good-natured rub on his chest and then visit with my lead dogs.

I lie in the snow next to Mustard to chat with him, like I normally do. He places his paw on top of my hand and stares intently into my eyes. I feel as though he knows everything that's in my heart when he assesses me like that. He sees my drive to stay independent and do things on my own without anyone asking me if I'm okay. He sees the fear too, that little voice inside wondering if I can run this race, if I can still do things on my own.

CHAPTER 12

The dogs are ready.

I keep them tied to the dropline of the truck while we're waiting our turn so I can avoid the chaos until the last minute. I try not to think about the fact I have no sunglasses. When I asked my family last night, the only pair anyone had belonged to Em, and I'm not taking hers. Maybe it will be overcast all day.

Guy appears beside me. He's wearing a normal anorak and fur hat. I guess the courier uniform was for the mass start.

"Oh, you *are* racing today," he says. "You know, if this weren't a stage-stop leg, I'd be way ahead of you by now. When I left, you were sleeping in."

"Is that right? Did you happen to notice I was still wearing my boots?"

"Now that you mention it, I did notice that. Good racing strategy. Did it get you up and running any faster?"

"You know you've started something, right?"

"No idea what you're talking about. Anyway, we should be safe today out on the trails."

"Safe?" My heart does a little thump at the thought of any dangerous obstacles that I'm not aware of.

"You remember, I read you about the wolf problem they used to have around here," Guy says. "The earless pig was just one instance."

I relax. "Right. I'll protect my ears."

"Another time the couriers were followed by the wolves. To keep them busy, they had to ditch the load of beef they were delivering to the camps."

I know what he's doing. "You think I'm going to be afraid of wild animals?" I say. "A little knot in my laces? You'll have to try harder than that."

Guy looks offended. "I'm sharing real history with you. I'm not making it up."

Four volunteers approach. "You're next to line up," one of them says to Guy. "We'll help you there."

As they head toward his team, I barely catch the satisfied grin

Guy throws me over his shoulder. "Happy thoughts out on the trail. Don't worry about the hungry, stalky wolves."

What a dork. I'm still smiling when some race officials approach me. "Morning, Miss Barney. We're doing spot checks for required gear."

"Right. It's all here." Thank goodness for my organization. I know where everything is in the bag. "Up here's all my cold-weather gear: parka, boots, spare mitts, socks. I have a compass, a cooker, fuel, food. All my first aid is here. That's for the dogs. Bootie bag, two sets each. Foot goop and ointments . . . oh, that's in case they get diarrhea." I pull things out for the officials, and they tick things off the lists on their clipboards.

"Along the side here I keep my ax, zip ties, and toolkit . . ." My stomach lurches. *Where is my toolkit?* I recall how I was dragged along the trail yesterday. Could I have lost it?

"Do you have the cable cutters?" one of the officials asks. "You need cable cutters to complete the check. Also, here's a tip: You should keep them handy in case you need them quickly. You never know what could happen out on the trail. You just can't predict it."

"Um. They were right here. Wait a minute." Why didn't I check my bag after I had the spill? I madly toss things out onto the snow, strewing all the gear from my perfectly packed bag around my sled.

That's when the girl from yesterday strolls by, the one with the dog tangle out on the lake. I recognize her bright pants.

"Hey," she says.

"Hey, uh . . . would you happen to have some spare cable cutters?" I ask, desperate. I hadn't seen her out on the trail again yesterday, and she's not out yet today, so I figure she must've scratched the race, which means she wouldn't need the cable cutters anyway.

"Sure." She spins and I'm shocked to see her run to the fancy dog truck in the parking lot. I can't read the name on it from here, but everyone knows what kennel that truck is from. Rodney Bowers has won every race he's entered this season. He's won the Wawa Gold every year for six years straight. I heard last night around the fire that a musher named Harper Bowers had the fastest time yesterday. *She's* Harper Bowers?

She comes back waving cable-cutting pliers.

I show them to the official, who ticks it off. "Good enough. That was a close one, eh?" She winks at me and turns to the girl. "Is your sled ready?"

"Yeah, I'll show you."

"Thanks, Harper," I call. "I owe you one!"

"We're even now," she says.

CHAPTER 13

We run along the ditch toward the tiny Batchawana Bay post office.

Each musher takes a turn getting his or her bag of letters stamped. The official race time starts up again after we're back on the trail, which is behind the post office on the snowmobile trail leading through the bush toward Pancake Bay. Volunteers and officials wearing chartreuse safety vests direct us.

After I hand over my bag of mail, I sit outside with my team and wait. They're uncharacteristically patient. Aspen climbs onto my lap and rests her head on my chest in a position that does not look comfortable. Sumo eats snow. Damage sadly inspects the booties on his feet. He knows he's not supposed to pull them off. Mustard sits, airplanes his ears, and mutters to himself.

"Are these your dogs?" a young girl about Emma's age asks.

She's perched just above me on top of the snowbank in a red snowsuit.

"Yup. Do you want to meet them?"

She shakes her head, shy. "Where are you from?"

"Soo, Michigan. What's your name? You live here?" I think of the cluster of houses that make up this small community. Imagine how it must be to grow up in a place like this, secluded, not many kids around to play with. It's a lonely way to live, so cut off.

"Kelly." The girl fidgets with her hat. "I've never been across the border."

"What? Well, you should go, the grass is still green over there."

Her eyes widen. "Really?"

"No, I'm kidding. We got snow same as here. In fact, I live outside the city, so it's pretty quiet where I'm from too."

Kelly nods thoughtfully.

Something about her seems so wistful and sad. I feel a kinship with her, living in a community at the edge of wilderness. Even though I'm in a bigger town, I know what isolation feels like.

I think of our yearly back-to-school shopping trip. Me, Mom, and Em usually go together and spend the day at the mall, trying things on, laughing, goofing around. It was the only day we were allowed to eat lunch at Cinnabon. It was one of the few things Mom had time to do with me too, rather than just Emma.

Because Em can't read the signs to know the right buses to catch, Mom will always need to drive her places. And read signs and labels for her.

But this past fall, I knew I wouldn't be able to read the labels either. I worried about looking at the tags on the clothes, about being in the right section, about finding Mom in a crowd. So I bailed and missed it. I miss a lot of things lately.

Kelly surprises me by pulling a letter from her pocket. "This is to my grandpa in White River. We don't see him much since our car broke. Can you take it with you?"

I nudge Aspen off my lap, stand, and then hesitate, not sure of the rules. *Can* I take it? She holds it out to me, but I can't tell what it says. I have to look closer. I glance around, then take her letter and bring it up to my face. It has a stamp and a full address. I'm still peering at the address when I hear a voice I recognize.

"Thank you. So, we go this way?"

I snap my head up. It's Guy on his way again. He's holding his mailbag and turning away from me to talk to an official. I can't tell if he saw me reading or not. What was I doing, trying to read with all these people around? *Careless!*

"So? Will you?" Kelly says.

I turn back to her. "I can, but I'm not sure it's going to get the DELIVERED BY DOG TEAM stamp. It's not in the special envelope."

"That's okay. I'll just tell him it was. The special envelope costs four dollars, so I couldn't get one. My grandpa has old letters in frames from when they delivered the mail by dogsled before, so he'd like this."

I smile at her then. "Okay. I'll make sure I mail it when I get there. Maybe I can get one of the dogs to step on it with goop on his paw."

She giggles.

"Ms. Barney!" An official is waving me up to the trailhead. She has my mail.

I stuff Kelly's letter in my sled bag and step on the runners. All the dogs stand. For a moment, I feel like a real mail courier from the old days leaving a village, all the people depending on me to deliver their news to family. About to forge ahead into unknown country.

"Have fun!" Kelly calls.

I turn and wave, and the image of her sitting alone on a snowbank, a solitary figure stark against the remote landscape, burns into my brain.

December 15, 1896

Dear Margaret,

Mr. Miron and I leave Sault Sainte Marie carrying a load of mail for another treacherous journey up the coast of Superior . . .

We are expected at the Michipicoten post in four days' time. I try to avoid my thoughts wandering to the question, If something were to happen out there, would anyone ever find us? I think I know the answer. We are truly alone.

Your loving brother, William

CHAPTER 14

O nce we hit the lake ice of Pancake Bay, I can tell I'm going to have to make some changes to the team.

Twix is suddenly unsure of all this space around her. She doesn't like the noises the lake is making, the eerie gurgling and thumping. I have to keep reassuring her there's enough ice between us and the cold black water below.

The actual trouble is that the snow cover on top of the ice is thin. If I stop and leave the sled, the dogs could pop the snow hook; there isn't enough for the hook to dig into. Without me on the brake, the dogs could take off. A musher's greatest fear.

I glance around helplessly. I can't tell how far away the end of the crossing is. Does the trail keep going all the way on to Montreal Harbour? I kick myself for not studying the map, but there were always too many people around for me to look.

"You're fine, Twix. I know it's kinda scary, but that's just the ice." Maybe she'll settle down.

Her tail goes up. She glances nervously back at me. I don't want to push her. It might sour her and make her decide leading isn't fun. Also, having a nervous lead dog is not good for team morale. They could turn on her.

I stop the team.

"All right, Twix." Her confidence is gone, and there's nothing for it. I'll have to risk it.

I take time to carefully kick in the hook, making sure it's solid. Still, I don't trust it. I scurry up to the dogs, giving them a steady stream of soothing words, my blood pumping.

I reach Mustard and Twix and stroke them while I try to come up with a plan. There's an endless list of options before me, all with various possible outcomes. Not every dog can lead. It takes self-confidence to run in front of all the other dogs. I have only so many dogs who can do it.

I can move Saga up in lead. I think she'd do well on the lake. But Twix and Aspen can't run together, two dominant females. Put Haze up with Aspen? But I don't want to put Twix in wheel either. She likes having room around corners.

"Good boy, Mustard," I say as I unclip Twix and bring her back to point position directly behind Mustard. My bare fingers feel the bite of the wind and freeze instantly. Quickly, I move Lizard back to run with Aspen and then shuffle up to Mustard again with a lunging Saga and hook her into double lead. She looks around proudly.

This is taking too long. Damage starts his screaming, frazzling my nerves. The whole team is yelling at me while I dart back to grab the sled. They're clearly saying, *We've noticed we're not running and we are totally ready to run, just so we're clear, one hundred percent ready, not currently running, so we can run now, just say the word, all set to stop not running any second now . . .*

I jump on the runners as the hook pops. Bending down to grab it, I laugh at the rush I feel as the dogs hit hyperdrive. It's as if they're all cheering Saga on in her new position. At this speed, I feel the icy temperature cut straight through me. It's windy and wide open out here. I work the drag brake, bringing them to a better pace. "Easy!" This is the race strategy Mom suggested. Conserve energy the first two days, then give them their heads. It's worked in the past. "Long way to go yet, you crazy heathens."

We end up staying on the ice for a couple more hours, so I assume we're crossing Montreal Harbour. Once the sun breaks through the clouds, I have to squint so hard I can barely see my dogs, never mind the scenery. It's like my eyeballs are being stabbed.

So I don't see the point where we hit the bush until we literally hit the hard ridges of ice that mark the spot where the lake ends and the trail begins. The sled teeters for a tense moment before I gain control. Then we fly down a nice trail, hard packed with a good base. It's a relief to be off the ice. We're going so fast, I hardly have time to register the trail marker as we zoom past it.

"Whoa! Whoa, guys! We missed something."

Asking the dogs to come around in such a tight space puts pressure on the leaders, so I get off the sled to do it myself. I take hold of the double lead between Saga and Mustard, turn them around, and march them toward the sled, past the team. Twix pauses to growl at Aspen.

"Hey!" I yell, and I drag her forward, picking up the pace. This is a prime opportunity for a tangle or a fight, everyone bunched together.

The sled pivots as I hop back on. We gallop along in the opposite direction. But I don't see another trail sign. Have we gone too far? Did we miss it, or should we keep going?

Now I'm the one who loses confidence. I can't tell where we are. I don't see any dog-team tracks in the snow, but I can't see that kind of detail anyway. And the dogs aren't telling me. They seemed content to go the wrong way back there, so I can't be sure if we've got the trail now.

We zip along, the runners hissing beneath my feet, trees whipping past. The dogs are all perfect, paced down to a ground-eating trot, about ten miles per hour. But are we going in the right direction? Indecision claws at me. My mouth is dry.

Suddenly, Mustard and Saga climb up a snowbank and disappear. The sled launches off the top. I hang on, knees bent, my guts left someplace in the air behind me. I crash down. Miraculously, I somehow land upright. We cross a snow-covered road that, also miraculously, has no traffic. The dogs sense that I'm hanging on to control by only a hair. They break into a lope. But the fact there were no officials at that crossing probably means we're not on the race trail. Unless that was an unused road, so they didn't need to be there?

The dogs' charging is finally slowed by a creek. It comes up so quickly that I'm sure Mustard didn't notice it until he was in it. He hates running through open water. Saga pulls him through. The runners clatter over icy rocks. My boots get wet, but I don't want to turn around in the middle of a creek, so we keep going.

Now I'm certain of it. We're lost.

A hot panic rises inside me. I twist my head from side to side, searching for some sign of which way to go. A ten-foot-high rock encrusted in ice on our left. Snow-covered spruce on our right. The sun's behind me, so we're still traveling west. Should we turn around? That wouldn't make sense. I need to figure out where we are! If only I had a cell phone with GPS, but race rules don't allow phones. Probably wouldn't get service out here anyway.

We hit a steep hill. As we climb, I take the opportunity to look behind us. But then I want to kick something in frustration. I can't see where we are, even from up here. For a moment, I want to give up. I feel immensely sorry for myself. It's so not fair that I'm losing my sight! That coil of terror and self-pity slithers up again. It would be easy to just wallow in this grief.

I can't let myself.

Sled-dog up, McKenna! Shake it off. Focus.

We need to go back. I stop the team again. As soon as I step off the runners, Saga drags Mustard around toward me.

"Saga, no. What are you doing?"

Mustard allows himself to be pulled. He's usually so good at staying out, but he creeps toward me. Now all the dogs try to crowd around me for comfort. Mustard's lost his confidence, or he's trying to comfort *me*. Somehow they can always tell when I'm stressed. I'm bringing everyone down with me.

I string them back out, taking time to visit with them and reassure everyone. They roll in the snow and grunt. I give Mustard a belly rub. Twix snags my pant leg from behind to drag my attention to her.

"Hey, don't rip them!" I say. "Yes, you're a good girl." I rub her chest and she flops over, splaying her back legs out wide.

I go back to the sled and smash off the ice that's formed on the runners so I don't slip. While I'm doing that, all the dogs perk their ears up at the same time.

They look to the left.

Dread hits me. Is it a moose? I was just thinking this is very moosey-looking country through here. Or maybe it's wolves?

"Stupid Guy," I mutter under my breath. Then I hear something.

A voice calls. "Gee!" The distinct sound of sled dogs panting reaches me. I hear them, but I can't see them. They sound like they're right on top of us.

"Hello?" I call.

"Whoa, Trucker," the male voice says. A pause. "*Aanii!* Hello!"

"Are you on the right trail?" I call.

"I think so. Where are—oh, there you are. Yeah, the trail is right in front of you."

I step off the brake, letting my team move forward, and a moment later we come out on a nice wide trail. I feel like a complete idiot, but I'm so relieved, I don't care.

"Oh, it's you, McKenna!" It's the big guy from the fire, Harvey.

"Hey, thanks, Harvey. We got turned around somehow. You know where we are?"

"Should be coming up to Sand River soon."

That tells me exactly nothing. "Great. Lead on!"

The chase helps Mustard find his confidence again.

CHAPTER 15

We eventually had to pass Harvey.

My team was too fast, especially going up hills, where Harvey really lagged. And now it seems like we've been climbing for hours.

I get off to run as much as I can, saving the dogs from pulling me. I think this gives me an edge over the older mushers. I love to run and I'm good at it.

I used to run on the cross-country team, but it's one of the things I quit this year. If I'm being honest with myself, I miss it. I miss the motion of just pumping my legs, one foot in front of the other. Mile after mile. It allows my thoughts to wander. It's weird that exercise can be described as relaxing, but that's how it works for me. So I'm grateful to be out here with the dogs. I can hold on to the handlebar and run beside the sled. Not that I need a guide dog. But Mustard is the closest thing to it.

The exercise is good. My boots crunch on the trail rhythmically. My breath pushes in and out in a cloud in front of me. No wonder the dogs are always so full of joy. When you're running, you can't look too far ahead. You can't look behind. You can focus only on the now.

At night I lie awake too often and worry about the future. About things like getting my driver's license. Am I going to be able to pass the test? What will happen when all my friends start driving and I can't? Will I be able to keep reading books? Should I learn Braille? What about going to restaurants and reading the menu? What kind of work can I do when I grow up? Would I even be able to move away from home and have a life of my own?

And I worry about Mom. She doesn't sleep when she's anxious. We all know when it gets bad, especially if Em has a test or something to do. Mom has a way of saying "I'm fine" with a certain tone in her voice that lets us all know she's not sleeping.

Piercing glare bounces off the snow around me and I desperately wish I'd brought spare shades. All this painful whiteness is killing me.

As we trot together, I can hardly see Mustard and Saga. But

their breathy panting is carried back to me on the wind and I can tell they're happy. We're all breathing the same winter air, smelling the same smells. Well, maybe not exactly the same. I can smell their dog odor. They can smell a lot more.

I heard once that a dog's nose reveals another world beyond what humans can see. I like that idea, imagining the dogs being able to know so much more than us. With their noses, they can see where people go, where they've been, what they're feeling. I wish my nose were as keen.

I stumble, and my focus returns. The task at hand is this hill. It demands my attention. It blots out the horizon. It blots out my fears of what lies near the end of this race.

The Cascades.

One foot in front of the other. Guy's great-great-grandpa climbed this hill with his mail. I wonder what's in the letters I'm carrying. I imagine delivering them to a town back then. Sitting with a hot cup of tea with some villagers around a fire and sharing the stories of my adventures out on the trail. How long has it been since I even sat with my own family around a fire?

We crest the hill, and there's the highway we've been warned about. I hear the wet sound of trucks going by as the trail runs next to it. Lizard glances at the passing truck but mostly keeps focused on pulling straight.

Volunteers are sitting on snowmobiles along the side of the trail. *Yes.* I'm on the right trail this time. One of them is waving and pointing left, the direction we're supposed to go to the crossing. If she could just point out every turn for me like that, the knots in my stomach would finally loosen.

"Way to go, Barney!" They cheer as I go by. Too late, I see someone had a hand out for me to high-five as I passed.

"Sorry!" People must think I'm stuck-up.

We follow the bend in the trail. My dogs hesitate in confusion over all the commotion. Several handlers jump in and grab sections of my gangline. "Ready? It looks good to go right now. We'll help you cross."

"Thanks!"

I'm so glad they're here. If they weren't, I'd be stressing about crossing this highway by myself. Mustard and Saga might decide they preferred to run on pavement for a while. Without snow for my brake to sink into, I'd have no control over where they took me. I wouldn't be able to stop the sled if they charged right down the highway. It sucks for the volunteers to have to sit out here all day, but they're definitely needed when a race trail crosses a road.

I hop off the runners and jog beside the sled as we cross so the smooth plastic underneath doesn't get gouged from the pavement.

From the horrible scraping noises, I'd say they're getting gouged anyway.

There aren't any cars. Thank you, northern Ontario, for quiet roads. It's all over in a blink. The handlers let go of my dogs; my dogs scuttle sideways to get away from them, and then they shake it off. They point their noses to the ground and get back to pulling. The noise of the crossing fades the farther we sink back into the trees.

I get back to running. *Crunch, crunch, crunch, crunch.*

I try to be like the dogs, thinking only of each step.

February 8, 2019

Dear Aunt Mae,

We're doing another race and I'm going to be the musher.
You know how much I love that. But this one we carry
letters, so I thought it'd be neat to send you one the
old-fashioned way. And check out the cool stamp. You
can never have enough sled-dog stuff. I'm working at the
grocery store this summer, so can't come visit. : (
But maybe you can ask my dad if I can come for March
Break? I miss your fab mall. Miss you too of course.

Love, Harper

CHAPTER 16

The dogs have been pulling for hours, eating up the miles.

I notice some of them pacing, rather than trotting, a sign they're resting muscles, so I step on the brake. "Whoa. Whoa, guys. Time for a snack."

I pull off to the side of the trail to make sure we're not in anyone's way. When I open the sled bag, the dogs look over their shoulders at me and start hopping. I grab the treats and walk down the length of my team, tossing frozen lamb snacks about the size of my fist. They snap them out of the air and hunker down to gnaw.

Once the snacks are gone, I tie off the snub line to a birch tree, stake out the leaders, and unclip tuglines. Aspen surprises me by trying to snag my glove. She's usually so serious. I give her extra attention, which leads to extra attention for Haze, and the two of them end up on their backs in a competition for cutest upside-down smile.

While visiting with the dogs, I attend to their feet. I check that their booties are on properly and not rubbing, replacing any that've blown a hole. I have to do this barehanded. The cold nips at my skin.

"Are you having fun?" I ask Saga. She sneezes right in my mouth. "Augh. Thanks." I spread her toes apart. "Look at this! No rubs or redness. No ice balls. Keep up the good work." I blow on my hands, trying to make them work again, then slip a fresh bootie on her.

One thing Mom has told me over and over: *No foot, no dog.* With all the miles these dogs cover each year, she's right about that. I stick my fingers in my armpits and look around.

It's dead quiet out here, no sounds other than the contented grunts of these goofballs rolling around. Even the trees are silent. No wind to rub their branches, not quite cold enough for the loud popping noise of sap exploding. In the winter, there are no birds singing, no leaves rustling. Just an absence of noise. A profound silence. There is nothing to hear but your own heart beating. The stillness is so complete, it makes your ears feel weird. It's my favorite season.

I take a moment to close my eyes, breathe in the fresh air, and blank my mind. The best part about being out here, just me and my dogs, is that they don't judge. When I'm out here alone with them, I can relax and not worry about anyone else.

Next, I root through my sled bag until I find the cooker. It's routines like this the dogs know. They see the familiar preparations and curl up on the line for a nap. Marathon dogs are conditioned to run for hours without getting tired, but they still need breaks, even in a race. A long-distance race is much different from a sprint. Out here, a musher needs to take the time to make sure the dogs' spirits are looked after as well as their physical needs. If they get bored or sour, they aren't much good in a team.

I toss a bootie into the outer bucket that makes up my alcohol cooker and light it up. Booties make good wicks. Into the inner pot, I dump the water that I put in my Thermos at the checkpoint this morning. Water will boil faster if I don't have to melt snow. My tea bags and sugar cubes are kept in a Ziploc inside a cup. As the water heats, I take a moment to relieve myself behind a tree. Soon I'm holding a steaming mug of tea between my fingerless gloves.

"Oh, thank God," a voice says. Harper pulls off behind me. "I'd love whatever you're having. My fingers have rigor-mortised to the handlebar."

Mustard's head pops up and I can tell he's studying my face for cues as to how we feel about this musher catching up to us. Satisfied with my vibe, he's content to sit and watch Harper's team with interest.

Her dogs are all obvious champions. Not that their looks matter in how well they run, but they're winning the intimidation factor. Every one of them is sleek, black, with perfect composition. They look like thoroughbreds. Next to them, my team looks like a group of misfit nags: Haze with her floppy ears, Saga with her spindly rat tail, Twix with her crabbing, sideways running. As if he knows I'm looking, Lizard lifts his head and displays his crazy teeth.

Harper settles her dogs and then trundles over. She plops down beside me, thrusting her hands out toward my stove. "Coffee?" she asks hopefully.

I pour the rest of the water into a spare cup and drop a tea bag in along with three sugar cubes. "If there's enough sugar in it, does it matter what it is?"

"Sing it, sister," she says. She takes the cup and then rummages in her pocket. She pulls out a Ziploc. "Carrot?"

I feel myself flinch and have to force a casual "No, thanks. I'm good." It's been a while since I've been exposed to carrots. Emma isn't allowed to eat anything with a lot of vitamin A in it because it could make her condition deteriorate, so we just don't have carrots in our house. I'd better be careful now too.

Harper munches and stares over the steam of her mug. "Why can't we do this somewhere a bit warmer, like Hawaii?"

"I don't think the dogs would like that." I love winter, but I'm used to my friends complaining about it every year, as if it's a big surprise that snow arrived. "You prefer cart training? I'm always excited when we can finally get on the sleds after it snows."

"I don't prefer any of it." Harper blows across her tea and hunkers down into her coat. "This isn't really my thing. You might have noticed."

"Isn't your kennel full of champions? I've seen your name everywhere."

"My dad's name, you mean. Mason, my younger brother, he loves it too. My dad couldn't wait for me to start doing the junior circuit. But I keep finding reasons to be busy. I couldn't come up with anything for this race, though, so here I am."

"You don't like running dogs?" I can't imagine it. "Why don't you just tell him?"

"I don't know. I can't."

"He must know you don't like it. It's not like you can fake that.

You don't want to tell him the truth? What's the worst that could happen?"

"You don't understand. He's got this way . . . he thinks I can do anything. My grades should all be perfect; my future will be perfect. You know when you're forced to live up to your parents' life-crushing expectations?"

I look at her with surprise. She has hidden depths. "Yeah, I think I know."

"Anyway, I don't like the cold. I don't like the speed. I'm just not good at it. It's scary and dirty and loud. And smelly! I mean, seriously, Titan's breath smells like garbage juice. It's so skeevy. All the dogs are too strong. They drag me all over the place. I can't control them. And I get stressed out with any obstacles. So I guess . . . no. I don't like running dogs," she says with a little laugh and a shake of her head. "Like, for instance that highway crossing back there. All I could do was stand on the runners and hang on. I hate stuff like that."

I grimace. "You didn't get off your runners when you went across the pavement?"

"Couldn't. I'd fall and lose them. You have no idea how strong these dogs are."

"Uh . . . yeah, I think I have some idea." I indicate my own team.

"Right. Sorry."

"Did you already change your runners?"

"What?"

I sigh and stand up. "Let's have a look at 'em, then."

We flip her sled on its side, and I run my hand down the ruined plastic. Then I realize what I'm doing. Harper's my competition. Letting her keep these runners on is going to slow her down, especially with her bulk. She's not light. She's even taller and broader than me. Her team has to pull against the drag. I should tell her the runners are fine.

Sliding my fingers along the deep gouges, I struggle with the dilemma. I glance at her dogs, eating snow, scratching their backs, legs kicking the air. Nope. I just can't leave them like this and make her dogs work harder. Plus, if I'm going to beat Harper, I'm going to do it without an advantage.

"You've got your spare set?"

"Um." She stares into her sled, shuffles gear around. "You mean these things?" She holds up a rolled set of quick-change runners.

"That's them. Should only take a minute." Bending to her sled, I pull out my knife. I pop the cotter pin loose from the front of the ski, pull out the pin holding the runner in place, loosen the plastic, and then slide it off the back of the track.

"It's stuck with ice," I explain as I bang it with the knife handle. "You're like my pit crew."

Once it's peeled off, I unwind her fresh runner and feed it into the track until it's all the way on. I pop the pin back in, secure it with the cotter pin, and then flip the sled to do the next ski. Once that's done, I raise my hands in the air. "And that's a new pit-stop record, folks, two point four seconds! The fans go crazy!"

Harper laughs, then points to something in the snow. She bends and picks up the mailbag. It must've fallen out when I turned the sled over. The letters are scattered all over the snow. I feel a twinge of panic at the thought of the same thing happening with my own bag.

"These things are a nuisance," Harper says as she kneels. I kneel with her and help scoop up the letters, none of which I can read. Harper pauses over one. "Hey, this one is from G. Desjardins. You think that's Guy?"

"Sounds like it." I have to stop myself from asking who it's addressed to. Wish I could somehow casually pull out Emma's magnifier. Helpful in occasions like this.

Thankfully, Harper is as nosy as me. She lingers over the envelope. "I wonder why he's writing to Amazon's contracting department. Think he's a corporate spy?"

"Yes, a spy," I say. "That makes sense, actually."

"I wonder if any of my friends mailed letters. I could be carrying them." She sifts through the envelopes, reading. "What about you? Did you read the mail you're carrying?"

"Uh, no."

"Any of your friends into this? Or do they think you're weird for running sled dogs?"

"No. I've been doing it since first grade, so my friends are pretty much used to me running dogs. It's not a big deal."

"Must be nice." Harper sighs. "I guess we shouldn't mess with these. Official mail and all that." She stands and stuffs the mailbag into her sled.

I peer at her. She's distorted. I wish the sun would go away. It's giving me a real headache. Harper notices me squinting. "Here." She passes me her sunglasses as if it's nothing. "I have a spare pair somewhere."

My breath hitches. A subtle relaxing all through my body. If only she knew how much this means to me! I take them from her, not even knowing what to say. When I put them on, I almost cry in relief.

"Thank you! This is . . . I really . . . thank you."

"So I should probably go out first, right?" Harper says.

"Yeah, okay."

As we pack up, my appreciation for Harper turns to envy. I

try to ignore it. Her dogs are faster; it only makes sense that she goes first. But I can't ignore the burning in the pit of my stomach. The unfairness of it, that Harper has two perfect eyes and doesn't use them to run all these fast dogs.

Why do I care so much when people waste their sight? I guess growing up with Em and seeing her loss of freedom along with her loss of vision makes me irritated by people who take perfect vision for granted.

I think about being at the fire last night when they were talking about the Cascades and I wondered if I should quit. But today, I'm not letting an icy cascade of doom stop me from finishing this. I have to do this.

Harper pulls away and I listen until I can't hear her anymore.

CHAPTER 17

Race trail, evening

As darkness falls, the bone-deep cold sets in.

Thankfully, we're protected by the trees as we run this trail. The temperature would feel different if we were still out along the north shore, exposed to the deadly gusts.

I breathe in, and my nose hairs freeze together. I blow out and smile at the white cloud rising in front of me. The air slices my cheeks. Northern lights shimmer above. It's turning into a glorious night.

Running at night, I don't have to deal with the sun glare. But the best time of day for me is evening, just before the sun goes down. After that, I have very poor night vision. Good thing the dogs see just fine in the dark. I flick on my headlamp as I rummage in the handlebar bag.

"Where is my neck warmer? I put it right here."

Sumo flicks his ears back but keeps running. I spy something white and pull out my spare scarf. It blocks the draft when I wrap it around my neck. Toasty and stylin', I get to enjoy the speed we're traveling now.

The dogs are flying. Running silent. They love running at this hour, when the smells are close to the ground. This night could not get any more perfect. Smooth trail without surprises. No glare. No ice. No dangerous highways. Happy dogs.

Sumo's ears flick back again and then Haze's and Lizard's. I glance back, and my headlamp illuminates the dog team behind us, an eerie line of bouncing, shiny eyes. A beautiful long string of them glows in the night. The reflective tape on harnesses also stands out in the light of my lamp.

The lead dog's eyes shine differently in that team following us. They're a weird greenish color compared to the others, which are clear and bright like jewels. I'll bet those weird eyes have a film over them. Even in the dark, Zesty is pretty distinct. I suddenly wonder what my eyes would look like in a reflection. Actually, no, human eyes are different.

I face forward again and some part of me deep down relaxes. It's nice to run with Guy near. Especially when he's behind me.

"Augh!" Something thumps me hard in the back of my head.

My foot automatically stomps the drag brake to slow us as I grab hold of my hat. I whip around. Did he throw something at me? Why would he do that?

"Hey!" I scream at him.

"What?" he yells back.

I face forward again, shining my headlamp through the team. My dogs are fine. They're running in sync, tugs tight. Suddenly, my head is knocked forward by what feels like a two-by-four. I jam on the brake again.

What the—I pull off my glove and reach my hand up to the back of my neck. It feels like blood between my fingers.

Guy's caught up to us now and I hear him yelling and pointing above me. I scan around and catch sight of something large winging above my head. It flies off and lands in a tree. I shine my light, and two orbs glow back.

"Watch out for the owl!" Guy is screaming.

I rub my neck again. "Owl?"

He stops his team when Zesty reaches me. "What are you wearing? Didn't you read the sign?"

"No!" *There was a sign?* "What sign?"

"It said to watch out for the man-eating owls along this trail. It said not to wear hats with pompoms. Tuck in any ponytails!"

Owls attack people? I glance down at my white scarf; it's

hanging out like a squirrel flying in the breeze. Perhaps I don't need a scarf. But what to do with my braids?

"Go away!" I yell at the owl still sitting on a branch. I peel off the scarf.

"Are you okay?"

"You mean besides the fact that I was just kicked in the head by giant freaking scissors?"

"Now, that's a good dog name."

I can't help laughing as I probe the back of my head. There's a tender spot and a bit of blood. "I'll live. Let's get out of here." I call the dogs. "Ready, Mustard? All right!"

We lope down the trail again. I didn't even hear that owl. My sense of hearing is usually so sharp. Yeah, except for when I'm stealth-attacked from behind by a demon with wings.

It nailed me right after I turned on my light. In case that had anything to do with it, I peel my headlamp off and stow it in my sled bag. I don't even care if I can't see.

"*Yip, yip, yip!*" I call, and they speed up.

Maybe we're past its territory now. Just as I think this, I feel the air move behind me. I shriek. I swing my arm above me and try to box the stupid bird out of the air. Guy is yelling.

And then I notice the icy cold ruffling through my hair. That owl stole my hat!

I brake and set the hook again. Now I need to find my spare hat. My shoulders are hunched in self-protection mode and I'm peering all around with wide eyes.

Guy has stopped his team. He walks up beside me.

"I'm going total ninja on this freaking owl if he comes back, I swear," I tell him. "Do you have a spare hat?"

He passes me the hat he's already holding, and something warms up inside me, despite the biting cold. Neither of us has a headlamp on, but in the moonlight peeking through the trees, I can see part of his expression. The shared experience of strange adventure binds us. I feel a pull toward him. Our eyes meet and we both break out in grins at the same time.

"Let's go," he says. "Bet you didn't believe you really *would* need to protect your ears out here!"

December 17, 1896

Dear Margaret,

We arrived at the Agawa post. I had a surprise awaiting me in the form of your letters! A mystery how they found me, but I am overjoyed they made it on the last boat of the season. Since the maximum load we carry in the sleigh is four hundred pounds, parcels and magazines must wait until the boats can bring them. Alas, any parcel you sent containing cookies is missing. The postmaster most assuredly ate them. Also missing is Anna's lucky tooth. I will write her and ask for another.

Your loving brother, William

CHAPTER 18

Gargantua Harbour checkpoint

The commotion in the community center overwhelms my senses.

I'm filling my bucket at the musher station. Not every race has this convenience, so I appreciate the laundry tubs set up for mushers to get hot water to soak their dog food. But there are people everywhere in here.

The sounds of cooking, talking, arguing, scraping chairs, people yelling to one another cross the room. Clothes and winter gear are strung up to dry in every available space, giving off a strong odor of dog and unwashed bodies. The long tables are full of diners clinking their plates and glasses. And the fluorescent lights glaring are too much after my evening run.

And you can tell you're at a dogsled race because even with all this commotion, from the hallway, incredibly, there's the sound of snoring. Several mushers are tucked into dark corners where there isn't much foot traffic. I almost trip over a pair of long sprawling legs, and then I recognize the anorak draped over them. How in the heck can Guy sleep with all this going on? And how did he get his chores done so fast?

I pause. Wait a minute. He's asleep?

I glance at his bootlaces. Nah, that's been done. Then I notice a clipboard hanging on the wall next to a coat rack. It has a black Magic Marker attached to it by a string.

Slowly, I uncap the marker and lean over Guy's head. Being this close, I can finally allow myself to tilt my head and look at him from the side of my vision. He has a nice face. It's angled sharply at his chin. His Adam's apple is pronounced. His mouth is usually a little sideways when he talks and smiles, but right now it's straight. His nose is crooked. His hair is dark brown and tucked behind his ears. My gaze ends at his eyebrows.

I reach out with the marker and touch the space between them. I wait, marker poised. He doesn't stir. With quick light strokes, I bridge his eyebrows together with a thick black line, giving him a unibrow. I'm considering horns on his forehead when his breathing changes. Hurriedly, I hang the marker back up, grab my bucket, and slip outside to water my dogs.

The trip from the community center to my dogs is

harrowing. I stumble on the holes and humps in the snow along the dark path while lugging my bucket of water. It's a miracle I don't wipe out. I'm wearing a good part of the water by the time I make it to the truck. The dogs are up and wagging their tails. My family must be having dinner in the community center because there's no one around. Good. Easier that way. And no risk of questions.

But as I find the bowls in the back of the truck, I feel some disappointment. I wish I could talk with them. I'd like to hear what Em thinks of all the excitement. I want to sit with my mom to ask her race strategies. I want to tell them about how well the dogs ran today, and I want to hear my mom tell me not to worry about the Cascades. That I'm a strong musher and I can do it. Even if she doesn't know about my sight challenges, I need that kind of reassurance. It's been a long time since we've talked, though. Really talked. I wouldn't even know where to start.

I'm scooping chicken water into bowls when someone walks up behind me. "McKenna, you were right." It's Harper. She sounds different. Excited.

"About what?" I drop a bowl in front of Lizard, and he gives me a big smile as he waits for me to fill it.

"I took—oh, that dog has a *lot* of teeth. Yeah, so I took your advice and talked to my dad about mushing. I sort of told him that I'm not into it. And you know what he said? I don't have to run any more races!"

"Really?" I look up from filling Lizard's bowl. "That's kind of . . . surprising. Are you glad you told him?" I imagine telling my parents what I need to tell them and once again feel a small envy for Harper and her uncomplicated life. It's not like I can just tell my parents the truth and everything will be fixed.

"Well, yeah, except there's one condition: I have to win this race. He said if I win this, he'll let me keep the purse and it can be my last one." Lizard slops bloody water over Harper's boots, and she moves out of the way.

"Oh." Maybe her life is more complicated than I thought. Why would her dad not let her stop unless she wins? What a jerk. "Well, you are winning, right? You've got a fast team. You could do it."

"Not anymore. They just put the times on the board inside. The top teams after today are Bailey Gant and Marc Bondar, then me, then Bernard Laberge. You and Guy are after that." She ticks the names off on her fingers. I feel a thrill that I'm in the top five.

"So for the next leg of the race, I have to go faster. I need to get a better time than Bondar and Gant. Can you, like, follow me and be my pit crew the rest of the way?"

"If I was fast enough to be able to follow you the whole way, I'd be trying to beat you," I tease.

"Right. Well, I'm going to have to get serious now. I just wanted you to know that I really need this to be my last race ever. Anyway, I'm gonna go hork down some lasagna before it's all gone. The community donated it for the *hero mail couriers*. Super-cheesy, right? But a big glob of cheese and noodles sounds delicious right about now. See you at the fire later?"

"Yup!"

Aspen is ignoring her water. I crouch down, hook a piece of chicken, and offer it with my fingers. She tentatively licks at it. A glob of fat next. She sucks it out of my fingers, then licks them clean. Soon she's got her face in her bowl and is drinking.

"Good girl," I say, stroking her back. Sometimes the dogs just need a dining companion to coax them.

I smile to myself as I watch her finish. Being in the top five is not what I expected when I signed up for this. Even though I've finished in the top five in past races, this is the longest and hardest race I've ever run. My chest swells with pride for my dogs. I can't wait to tell Em and my parents.

January 10, 1897

Dear Uncle William

We got a letter from you! It took over a month to reach us here in Toronto. Killarney sounds very exciting. I will tell you a secret. You are my favourite uncle. Do not tell Uncle Stephen. When I grow up I want to go on adventures like you, but Mama says that is not for young ladies.

Love Anna

CHAPTER 19

Once the dogs are settled, I head back to the center to find my family. But when I step inside, I hear their angry voices and it makes me pause by the door. They're at the first table and I can feel the tension from here. I want to turn around and leave.

"I'm very sure, Beth," Dad is saying when I join them.

"Sure about what?" I ask, wishing we weren't in the middle of a community center with all these people around. "What's going on?"

"Nothing," both my parents say at the same time.

"Some of us are being so pigheaded they don't see what's right in front of them," Mom says.

I look at Em, but with the lighting in here, I can't see her face clearly. Nonchalantly, I get up and move to the chair next to her.

"Everyone is doing fine where they are," Dad says.

And then I know what they're talking about. A glance at Em confirms it. She knows too, even though they think they're being so stealthy.

"Remember, you've got to let them fail," Dad continues. Seriously, does he think we're so stupid that we don't know what they're discussing?

"Well, that's not an option," Mom snaps. "I'm just saying, this week proves my point."

Her point is that she wants to pull Emma from school so she can homeschool her. We heard them discussing it a few months ago. I'd been in Emma's room when their whispers reached us from the kitchen.

After Emma had fallen down the stairs two years ago, everyone moved bedrooms. Despite Dad insisting, "You can see this stair, right, Emma?" she couldn't see the contrast between the last two steps and the floor. It's not as though she got hurt, but from then on, she was confined to the main floor unless she was with someone. I even dragged my mattress off my bed and down the carpeted stairs—*thump, thump, thump*—and wedged it next to the bottom stair. I thought I had solved the problem. I was twelve.

So Em's room is in my parents' old room on the main floor down the hall from the kitchen. Even if you've got the door partially closed, if your parents start to whisper, it's amazing how your hearing instantly becomes supersonic.

"She wouldn't have to worry about getting around the school anymore," we'd overheard Mom say. "Or about getting the right books or organizing her homework. Those teachers don't have time to help her, and they don't understand her needs. I could join the homeschooling association and learn—"

"No way!" Dad sounded like his jaw was clenched. "She's going to school like a normal kid."

"Dan, she's not . . ."

If she says Emma isn't normal I'm going to slam the door, I thought.

"It was because of your stubbornness and your refusal to accept that there was something wrong that we waited so long to take her to the doctor," Mom hissed.

"*My* stubbornness? Who's the one who packs her backpack for her every morning and reads things to her even though we've been told that she needs to do all that herself?"

"If she's at home, at least we wouldn't have to worry about her all day."

"Who's worried? I'm not. Emma isn't. The only one worried is you. You're making this into something it's not. She's going to school. End of discussion," Dad said then.

"End of discussion," Dad says now in the community center.

Mom takes the Thermos that she was pouring something into and places it on the table. She stands and walks away. I glance at Emma and see her eyes shine with tears.

Inside, I seethe quietly for Em. For me.

These arguments are getting old. And they've gotten worse. I would have thought that, with time, they'd both come to work together, but it seems to have only pushed them apart. More and more I feel like this family doesn't have room for another case of Stargardt disease.

December 20, 1896

Dear Margaret,

I must tell you of the heroics of my companion
Mr. Miron and his pole, which he fashioned from a
length of spruce to pry at the sleigh in the slush.
Unfortunately the ice gave way underneath me. I
was at once plunged into water so cold that I could
scarcely take a breath. I do not think I uttered
a yell, but Raymond heard the splash and fetched
that long pole. He crawled over the ice so that I
could take hold, and, somehow, he plucked me out,
which was well since I hadn't the strength to do it
myself. I was even too cold to walk. Raymond said,
"Mon dieu!" and proceeded to pull me to an island
and built a fire.

Your loving brother, still alive, William

CHAPTER 20

Mushers are drawn to the nightly bonfires like parka-clad moths.

All the same young crew from last night are here except for Guy. I hold my hands out to the warmth of the flame and listen to the conversations around me. I want to soak up this sense of community. I want to forget about my own problems for five minutes.

Laughter nearby startles me. I hear Guy's voice. "Yeah, yeah. I got carried away with the makeup. Trust me, I've been hearing about it all night."

He sits beside me on the bench. "There you are, enemy mine. You wouldn't happen to know why I'm turning Klingon, would you?"

"It's a good look for you. Very bold statement."

"Mmm." He rubs at his eyebrows with a finger. "I think I'll keep it. The vet really likes it too. Didn't know it would be so popular with the ladies."

"The ladies? What are you, forty?" I laugh. "How did your vet check go?"

Guy turns serious. "I just dropped Muskrat and Icon."

"Oh no! What happened?" It's always painful to leave dogs behind. I think of my own vet check. I'd asked her again to look at Aspen's shoulder. She's the only dog I have to worry about. Well, I'm always worried about Sumo, but not in the same way. The vet said my dogs were strong and healthy, even Aspen. They all still have so much heart in this, and I was proud the vet noticed.

"We talked it over," Guy says. "The vet didn't think I had to drop them yet, but it's better for the dogs. Muskrat's got an abrasion between her toes on her left front foot. Now her pads are red and starting to swell. It was totally my fault. The snow was so grainy. I should've been quicker to replace the bootie she blew."

Guy worries at a thread from the hem of his anorak. "I massaged her feet and I've got them all wrapped now. She'll get the royal treatment riding the rest of the way in the truck with Dad and his girlfriend."

"What about Icon?" It's a tough decision to drop any dog, but especially a leader.

"He's got a stomach bug that's not going away. I think he's lost weight. Seems sluggish. If I'm not careful, that could spread through the team, right?"

There's such angst in Guy's voice. I nod in empathy.

"Icon's good for Zesty's confidence in lead," he continues. "She's always leaning on him, like she's soaking up his courage, you know? But if he's not having fun anymore, I'm not asking him to keep racing. Now I have to use Diesel up in lead. I should have brought more leaders in my race team in case this happened. But at least I still have Zesty."

"How do you run with a blind lead dog?" I can't help but ask.

"You know the connection you have with your leaders?" Guy says as I see Harvey walk over to us. "It's even stronger with her. She doesn't let the fact that she's blind stop her—what? Oh, thanks." Guy takes a bag from Harvey, pulls out a piece of red licorice, and passes the bag to me.

I pull out one piece, the sweet smell of the candy familiar and calming, then pass the bag on to the next person. When I take a bite, the licorice is cold and hard. I hold it in my mouth to thaw a little before chewing.

"The best thing about animals," Guy says, "is they don't feel sorry for themselves. Zesty loves to run in lead. But she has to listen to me because she can't see where she's going. She has to trust me more, so we have an even closer relationship. And she's so confident up there. She understands me better than any dog I've ever run."

I think of the bond I have with Mustard, which is sort of the same thing as what he's talking about, just in reverse. I'm the one who has to listen to Mustard more. "I know what you mean."

We chew our licorice in silence. I search for something to cheer him up.

"Do you have any more old letters?" I ask.

"From Grandpa Desjardins?" Guy asks eagerly. He plucks the little book out of his pocket. "In fact, I do. Let's see what the mail couriers are up to."

As he reads, I notice how nice it is to be sitting side by side feeling the warmth from the fire and the warmth from Guy's shoulder next to mine.

Soon it begins to snow. Guy tries to protect the pages, but they're getting wet. After he's finished a dreadful story about the couriers falling through the ice, he tucks his book away.

"More snow," he remarks, tilting his face up. "Did you

know Lake Superior gets the most snowfall of anywhere in Ontario?"

"No, I didn't. Good thing I have my walking encyclopedia beside me to keep me current."

"Just saying, you never know what kind of dangerous adventures you could run into out there."

CHAPTER 21

The mushers sleep in a prospector tent set up next to the community center.

There are cots inside lined up in two rows with very little light. I slip in and quietly find the cot I picked out earlier and claimed with my sleeping bag. It's closest to the door and breezy, but I don't have to stumble or trip over anyone to get to it.

The cot creaks and my bag crinkles as I lie down. Earlier, I left my boots here to dry, taking out the liners and wearing my camp boots to go out to the fire. I lean over and put my hand in to check them, muffle a surprised noise, and whip my hand back out. Then I press my lips together and gingerly feel inside again. There are small hard things like pebbles in the bottom.

I stick my nose into my boot and sniff. Yup. Dog kibble.

Someone has been messing with my boots again, and he

probably looks like a Klingon. I dump out both boots and then shake my head. Amateur.

I hear the murmuring and shifting of sleeping mushers as I stare at the ceiling. I glance at my watch. In only five hours I have to get up to water the dogs and prepare for the day's race. And I'm already exhausted from the past two days. I need to be rested for tomorrow.

Tomorrow is going to be the big test. A hundred and thirteen miles without a stage stop like this one. A long time without help if I need it. The worst part is the Cascades. After the final checkpoint, I'll still have to somehow make it through the Cascades before I get to the finish line. Before I can hand over my mailbag.

I keep imagining how it will feel to turn to Emma and say, "See? I'm fine." In my mind, it's a great moment.

I close my eyes and try to ignore all the strange smells and sounds of this place. I miss my bed. Suddenly, I miss all the familiar comforts of home. I miss the security of knowing exactly where everything is. I miss knowing what obstacles I'll have to face the next day. Here, everything is unknown and new. As I toss in the narrow cot, my thoughts are interrupted by a noise outside.

I hear a single, long howl.

It starts low and rises, beautiful and lonely and haunting. In the next instant, the howl is joined by several other voices. They all have different tones and pitches but somehow, it's harmonized. The song builds, with more and more howls joining in until every single dog in the parking lot is a part of it. There are over a hundred dogs out there, all throwing their heads back and singing their hearts out.

Their voices weave in and out with one another's. The howls rise and fall; some voices are rich and full, others are squawky and hoarse. With so many voices, the sound is deafening. Thunderous. It vibrates all through my body like drums in a drumming circle. It feels ancient and raw and true. It reaches into my soul and touches me, wraps me up in its expression of unity and joy. The whole camp has paused to listen. The dogs have cast a magic net and joined all of us together.

The howl rises in a crescendo. One pack of dogs devoting their entire spirit. There is nothing but the song. I let it seep into me. I can hear it with my heart.

Slowly, the noise begins to fade and I come back to myself. Once again I'm lying on my cot in the middle of a musher tent. The last note of the song ends. Everyone pauses as it hangs in the air. I imagine it drifting off into the night sky like the fog of frozen breath.

Conversations from the fire pit start back up and reach me,

muffled by the canvas of the tent walls. But now, somehow, I don't feel so alone.

I close my eyes and sleep.

DECEMBER 20, 1896

DEAREST ANNA,

FINALLY I HAVE TIME TO WRITE AS WE REST HERE FROM OUR LAST LEG. WHEN I COME HOME, WE WILL GO SEE THE DIVING HORSE. I WISH I COULD TAKE YOU TO SEE THE RACES HERE ON THE FROZEN MASSEY RIVER. A PET MOOSE RACES THE HORSES! REPORTEDLY HE IS THE FASTEST TROTTER THERE EVER WAS! . . .

I AM BUSY FEEDING AND CARING FOR THE SLED DOGS AND ATTENDING THE SLEIGHS. WE COVER THEM WITH TARPAULINS, EMPLOYING A CRISSCROSS SYSTEM OF STRAPPING, SO IF THEY ROLL, THE MAIL DOES NOT GET WET. I THINK OF YOU EVERY DAY AND LOOK FORWARD TO YOUR NEXT LETTER. IT HAS MADE MY WORK LIGHTER.

LOVE, UNCLE WILLIAM

CHAPTER 22

Stage three: Gargantua Harbour to White River
113 miles

Because of my team's fast time on the last leg, we have to start near the end of the pack today.

The first few hours I spend just passing other teams.

"Trail!" I call again and again. Mustard and Twix behave themselves up there and don't tangle with the other dogs.

Some people who don't mush think it's crazy to trust any dog so much, to depend on him. But I know Mustard. I know his mind. And he knows what I want. I trust him to make a clean pass.

But some dogs are sneaky. They know what they're supposed to do and yet constantly try to get away with not doing it. Lizard can be like that when he's in a mood. You have to watch those kinds of dogs all the time. They're like the class clowns, always spending energy testing how far they can push it. But dogs like Mustard are known as *honest* dogs. I can depend on him doing his best up there, even though I can barely see him.

Again, I wish I could've studied a map of where we're going. Harper had called me hardcore when I admitted I hadn't really looked at the race route, and I sort of agree with her.

My concern about it had made me risk a peek last night when I pretended to drop something in front of the posted map at the checkpoint. I'd bent down, then brought my face next to the map. I had time to see the red line running the north shore of Superior but not any details. When I stood, I thought I caught sight of Guy watching me.

I adjust my sunglasses to let out the steam from my sweat that's fogging them up. Thank God for Harper giving me her spare. I'm still wearing Guy's hat too. It smells like boy. When I rub at an itch on my temple, something scratches me. I peel off the hat and feel something hard and sharp that I'm pretty sure is frozen snot, but at this point, I'm not sure if it's mine or Guy's. I shrug and stuff the hat back over my greasy hair.

We still haven't come across Guy. He went out not far ahead of me. Harper went out behind me. Being in the leader group, she's been going out near last every day.

I'm busy straining to see ahead—searching for Guy, if I'm honest with myself—when I notice the trail getting narrower. Clumps of alder and slender birch have grown in and made a tunnel. The trail is icy here. The runners clatter noisily over the ruts.

One of the ruts is deep. My sled's ski hits it, catches an edge. It shoves the sled onto its side. I heave it back. We pound into another hard rut. The sled is wrenched over to the other side. A sharp, knobby branch grabs my sled bag, pushing until we break free. On its side, the sled skates and rattles across the icy ruts like a runaway lawn chair in a stiff wind. Grunting, I finally wrestle it back upright by grabbing the stanchions and heaving with all my strength. The trail is sloping downhill. The dogs speed up.

I work the brake. "Easy, easy."

The points of my brake dig in. But the trail is furrowed, minimizing the effect of the brake. I stand on the drag. We don't slow down. The momentum is a rolling barrel, and now the dogs are in full charge. All I can do is hang on. We hit a bump; the sled goes airborne, then slams down hard. We crash into another rut and keel sideways again. This time, I throw the sled on its side on purpose to slow us down. I drag along the ice, one leg bent and one stretched out behind me. I skid on the side of my thigh, sparing a thought to my brand-new shell pants. I hope they don't rip. I don't even have another pair and it would be highly embarrassing to show up at checkpoints with ripped pants.

The trail levels off and I fight the sled back upright again. It takes all my concentration to keep us under control.

I'm drained and exhausted by the time we break out of the tunnel. Sweat plasters my hair onto my forehead. I'll be happy if I never see another alder again in my life.

The trail flattens as we run across a frozen bog, the skis making a soft sound over the snow. The smell of muskeg reaches me. Frozen cattails whip by. Soon we're back into the balsam trees on the other side. I don't notice the other team pulled over until we're beside them. I step on the brake.

"You good?" I ask. It's Harvey.

"Sure," he answers. He's sprawled out on his back on top of his sled bag. It looks like a fantastic idea. I'm so tired, I think about resting here too.

Owooooo, Mustard says. Sumo slams into his tugline, trying to pop the hook. The dogs are still full of jazz. Not a good time for a break.

"I better go. I'll see you later," I say.

"Yeah, your team is pumped! Go get 'em," he says.

Pride warms my belly. My dogs are strong and fast. I'm still shocked we're in the top five. I'm starting to believe we can actually do this — as long as we can make it through the Cascades.

For the next hour the trail is better. I relax and enjoy myself out here. We cruise over the punchy snow with a *sssshhhh*. The best part: The sun is covered, so the light is flat. Moody overcast with a low ceiling. Getting darker, actually. And the wind has picked up, dragging loose snow over the surface with a hiss.

I still don't see Guy, but I feel as if we've passed almost every other team. Sumo and Damage are both dipping snow, signaling they need a break. They're either bored or thirsty.

I call out, "Whoa," and sink the hook. I hop off the runners and shake out my arms. The dogs roll around, scratching their backs with glee. While they're busy, I move to my sled bag to get a drink. But when I dig into my bag to find my Thermos, I see a tear in the sled bag along the Velcro closures. Two of the Velcro pieces ripped off and opened the top of the bag, exposing all the contents.

I curse. Is my Thermos still in there? I root around until my hands find the smooth round container. I pull it out and take a long chug. As I drink, I inspect the tear, bending over to look at it.

How did this happen? Not to worry, I have bungee cords

along the bottom front of the sled. I can close the bag with that. Make sure I don't lose anything.

I freeze. A horrible thought occurs to me. I claw through my gear. My fingers search for the metal grommets, the canvas. *Where is it? Is it here? Please be here.*

But it's not here. It's not anywhere. My legs lose strength and I sit hard in the snow. Somehow, somewhere on the trail, I've lost the mailbag.

Emma's letter is gone.

Maybe it's at the checkpoint. Did I have it when they checked my sled for gear? I don't even know. Or maybe one of my parents took it out for some reason and forgot it in the truck. Who am I kidding? There's little chance of that. I have to face the fact that I've left it behind on the trail.

What am I going to do? I wrap my arms around my middle and bend over, trying to breathe. All the mail from Emma's entire class is gone. Emma's wish for better awareness of Stargardt disease and more research, gone. The opportunity for media coverage. Gone. Gone. Gone.

How could I lose all the mail? The poor mailbag that I've sworn to protect. What other letters was I carrying that aren't going to be delivered? Are they going to sit out all winter, perhaps found almost destroyed in the spring? Guilt claws my throat at the thought of all those people who wrote letters that won't reach their destination because of me.

But the vital thing that has sucked the breath out of my lungs —our secret pact. I can't deliver Em's letter. *I've failed.*

My own words to Em taunt me: *If I don't deliver your letter, we tell them.*

I'm not ready! My parents *can't* know yet.

And what am I going to say to the officials about the mailbag? What if I don't tell them? What if I don't let anyone know until I get across the finish line? My mind spins trying to come up with a new plan.

What if . . . if I can't deliver the mail, what if I *win* the race? I could stay quiet about the mail until the end. And if I win, it would prove that I can do anything. It would show Em that someone with Stargardt disease can do anything.

Can I win this race? Prove I'm capable even with a sight impairment? If I do win, I'll be ready to tell my parents. I'll be ready to get tested and have the truth come out. If I win, my parents won't be able to make me stop running dogs. They won't be able to treat me like Emma.

I bolt straight up. I tie the bungees around the sled bag to close it, full of new resolve. "Okay, guys," I say to the dogs. "No time to waste."

We're here to *win*.

February 1, 2019

Attention: Amazon Contracting Department

Desjardins Delivery, our courier business, is the perfect opportunity for you to expand your services in northern Ontario. We are local, we've been in business for four generations, and we are fast. We're so fast, our dog team has just won a historic courier race, the Great Superior Mail Run (I'm pretty sure this will happen), making our name famous and synonymous with speed. What more could you ask for in a courier? Please consider Desjardins Delivery for your northeastern contract.

Sincerely, Guy Desjardins

CHAPTER 23

The wind hits us as we follow the trail out of the trees and onto the ice of Old Woman Bay.

I'm balancing on the runners while trying to crack open my string cheese. The wrapper is frozen, my fingers are frozen, and my ski goggles fog up as I bend over the package. What is this made of, titanium? I can't even see what I'm doing so I don't dare use my knife.

Another gust blasts me just as I rip the package open. My cheese goes flying off to freedom. "Son of a monkey!"

Where did this wind come from? It blows back Mustard and Twix. They hunker down and dig into it. Twix seems on board now for leading on the ice, so I leave her be. "Good dogs!"

As we head out into the bay, the wind builds.

I peer through my goggles and try to differentiate between

shadows and snow snakes blowing across the trail. Saga and Haze stumble from the force of the gale, but they put their heads down and charge into it. Their determination makes me love them so much my chest hurts. They're epic-brave. No matter what's thrown at them, they don't think about what they can't do, just what needs to be done, and then they do it.

The ice creaks beneath us. Crossing the ice is different here than it is on a small lake. On Lake Superior, the ice cover shifts endlessly. It's never still. It expands and contracts. It buckles and flexes. I can feel the vibrations through my feet. It's a weird, scary feeling, but I remind myself that the ice is three feet thick. We're not going to break through.

A stray thought hits me like ice water — where exactly on this frozen stretch of lake were the couriers when they fell through? I grit my teeth and plan to bean Guy with that book next time I see him.

Some of the noises the ice makes are like what you'd hear in a Star Wars movie: *pew-pew-pew*. But it also lets out long eerie moans. It's a tough thing to get used to. The dogs don't seem to mind as much now, though. They only twitch their ears.

Great angry gusts wallop my anorak. When I raise my arm to wipe off my goggles, my sleeve flaps. Not that I can see the trail markers anyway, but I'm worried. It's been a very long time since the last marker. I tuck my neck farther down into my scarf and peer around into the white. *Are we still on the trail?*

The sled bumps over the hard ridges on the surface of the frozen bay. Some of it is smooth snow, but sometimes we clatter over slabs of ice like broken patio stones. All I see as we race over it is ice and snow and weird sculptures shaped by the wind and random mounds of frozen slush as big as bicycles. Sharply jutting spikes of ice thrust upward. It's like the moon out here.

I study Mustard. His ears are forward, and his tail is straight behind him. He's confident and sure, focused on what's in front of him. We must still be on the trail.

Twix is the first to signal there's something ahead. Then all the dogs' ears prick up. I peer into the snow with trepidation. *What now?*

A shadow comes into focus. I breathe a sigh of relief when I recognize the crazy French boy on the runners. He has a habit of rocking from foot to foot that's unmistakable.

My dogs slow down. I brake as I realize that Guy has pulled off the trail in the lee of some kind of ice wall.

When the ice shifts, sometimes it cracks and gets pulled apart. It makes fissures wide enough that steam from the cold water beneath escapes up into the air. Other times, the cracks are pushed closed. When the two chunks of ice meet, they've got nowhere to go but up. They're shoved into the air with relentless force, creating walls of ice.

I tuck in next to Guy behind the ice wall. It towers above us, maybe two feet taller than me. It's at least a foot and a half thick and it's covered in snow on one side.

"I've got to replace booties. This ice is shredding their feet," Guy says. We're out of the worst of the wind here, so I can hear him clearly enough to tell his voice is tight.

"Go ahead if you want," he says. His shoulders are bunched together. I watch as he savagely roots through his sled bag.

I find a crevice in the ice to wedge my snow hook into and check my dogs' feet as well. Everyone still has booties except Damage. He holds his feet up impatiently while I bend over him. I have to bring his feet right up in front of my face to inspect each foot. Then I smear goop between his toes before slipping new booties on. I cinch them around his ankles with the Velcro tab. The wind is murder on my bare fingers.

In the ten minutes or so it takes for Guy to bootie and check his dogs, the wind doubles. As soon as we peek out from behind our ice block, it hits us full force. The air is choked with swirling, sharp snow crystals. It's a desert-scape of white.

"You think we should stay here?" Guy asks.

We peer around the ice to gauge the wind. Is it going to slack off or build? Is it much farther to the shelter of shore?

This is a bad place to stop. It's cold and exposed, and the dogs are not relaxed. I'm not thrilled about waiting here much longer.

"Let's just go," I say. "Before the dogs balk. We should keep moving." I've heard enough of Mom's race stories to know that once momentum is gone, the dogs can sometimes decide they'd rather hunker down. We'd be stuck if that happens. In this tiny patch of calm in the center of a blow.

Guy nods tersely and calls up his team. They shake off and head out as I watch. Knowing how much I depend on Mustard up there, I can't understand how Guy can rely on Zesty to go the right way. I can see she's joyous and driven, but she's different than a regular leader. How does he trust a *blind dog?*

My dogs follow Guy's team eagerly. Being the chase team takes the pressure off my leaders. To be fair, we should take turns. But I don't think I should be leading.

Now that we've started out across this bay, we're committed. The scariest part is that I can't stop in this wind. If I need to fix a tangle in the dogs or move one of them, I can't leave the sled. The hook won't set, and I'm afraid the wind will rip the sled away, pulling all the dogs with it. And if I stop, the dogs are likely to curl up immediately and refuse to start again. I just have to hope they keep moving.

It isn't long before the howl of the wind is all I hear. I can't even make out the rumble of the runners over the ice. I haven't noticed how much I rely on my hearing these days. But now that it's gone too, I feel even more vulnerable.

Twix is so little she gets blown sideways. I can barely see her through the spindrift. The wind picks up the top crust and blows ice pellets into our faces. I fight to see ahead.

Suddenly, we smash into something. The dogsled slams to a halt, jerking my wheel dogs back. I hear my own shriek as I'm ripped from the runners.

And I fly off the sled.

When my mind catches up with what happened, I sit up, searching for my dogs. They've gathered around me, trying to get as close as they can. My head throbs. My team is okay. I'm okay. *What did I hit?*

My sled is wedged against an ice ledge. There's a crack across the trail that's shifted together and made a shelf of ice as high as my shin. I didn't even see it.

Guy is abruptly looming over me. "Can you walk?"

"I think so." He helps me stand, and I notice he's secured both our teams, driving the snow hooks into the ice. I must've hit my head when I flew off the sled and blacked out for a moment.

Both of our teams have now curled up against the wind like snowballs. This is a dangerous place to stop. We have got to keep going.

"How did you miss this thing?" Guy yells. "I swear, sometimes you remind me of Zesty the way you . . ." And then I see him answer his own question. He stares at me hard. "How much can you see?"

I don't even argue with the certainty in his expression. He *knows*.

I wait for the dread to come, now that someone has guessed my terrible secret after I've spent all this time trying to hide it. The emotion washes over me, just not the kind I was expecting. Relief rushes in and threatens to take over my head. *I don't have to pretend anymore.*

I push it back. Not the time to fall apart. We're in trouble out here.

"It depends," I admit. "Right now, not much."

CHAPTER 24

S tay close. Follow me."

It takes us a while to call up the dogs. But they finally agree to start out again. My lead dogs are now running as close to Guy as they can. Mustard is practically on his boots.

My whole body tenses and quivers. We have to get out of here. The gale howls into my ears, filling the world. It is relentless, forcing its way into every crevice of my clothing. It blasts my exposed skin raw. I've never been so cold. I'm exhausted just trying to stand upright. I don't even know how the dogs are running.

Guy is yelling something, but I can't hear what. He's waving his arms and pointing at me.

My heart pounds. I peer ahead, straining to see if we're about to crash into another ledge of ice. Mustard and Twix hop into the air at the same time. And then Lizard and Damage do the same.

And then Saga and Aspen. Two by two, they all leap like they're doing the wave at a sports stadium.

Two things happen simultaneously. I become aware of the steam billowing into the air and I hear the runners slide off the ice. They make a peculiar noise. Water gushes over my boots just as the sled pops back onto a solid surface.

My knees feel like putty. They barely hold me up. We just went over a crevice in the ice. I couldn't even see it because of my faulty depth perception. It could easily have been wider, in which case we'd all be at the bottom of Lake Superior right now. I feel woozy and ill with how close that was.

What would have happened if we were out here on our own? Mustard would've been in danger up there without guidance. We all would have.

What was I thinking, trying to run this race?

We pass another large slab of ice jutting sideways about neck-high. It's absolute madness to be out here. We could be blown off the ice and fall into a crevice, hit an ice slab and be guillotined. We have to get to shore and find shelter.

Ooooooooo! Mustard's questioning my sanity. He keeps up his talking until it's all one big scream, getting louder and louder.

"Yeah, I know, Mustard," I scream back.

Other dogs have joined him. Before I know it, my whole

team is screaming while they're running. The dogs are never vocal while they run, only at hookup. Running is always silent. But we've never run in wind like this before. They're scared.

"You're okay!" I call to them. "We'll find shelter once we get to shore. Just keep going."

And they do. They keep trying to run in the wind. They might think I'm crazy, but they trust me.

An odd feeling prickles up my spine. I sense something closing in, like when a ball is coming at you and you don't see it but you throw your hands up anyway. In the next instant, the shoreline is suddenly beside us. The cliffs tower above, looming. But they don't shelter us from the wind like I thought they would. Ice pellets are still hurtling through the air around us. The wind shrieks across the bay and smashes into us.

Everything is a fight. With every step, every action, we push back against the insane gusts that are whipping us to the bone.

What are we going to do? My dogs are faltering. Twix has lost confidence again. She keeps glancing back for reassurance. I scan around frantically for a place to shelter from this storm. All I see is white. Everything inside me is shouting that we must get out of this wind.

Now!

And that's when it happens. I don't see it. Guy doesn't see it.

Zesty certainly doesn't see it. But Mustard does. He veers closer to one of the ice walls clinging to the cliff. And when I strain to peer through the blowing snow, I finally see it too.

"A cave!" I yell.

Guy glances back and I wave my arm and point. "A shelter!"

We head toward it. The dogs instinctively know it's going to get them out of this wind. I tumble off the sled and lurch toward the opening, my team following behind.

The massive sheet of ice coating the cliff face is so thick, it's formed a solid wall. Gigantic frosted fangs hang all the way to the ice of the lake. There's a natural opening like a gaping mouth where the cliff overhangs and the ice hasn't covered it. As soon as I get behind the ice wall, the relief from the wind is profound. I almost fall over from the absence of it. I can breathe again.

I peer around the dim interior. My ears ring in the muffled silence. The cave goes back farther than I can see. It's completely protected on all sides with walls made of blue ice. They feel like frozen plastic under my bare fingers.

Unlike the ice formations on the first day, which were created by wind, these were made by water running down the rock. On the far left wall, icicles hang like stalactites so low they almost touch the floor. The rest of the roof is high enough I can stand up.

The dogs sniff at the ground, which is a mix of rock and ice. I grab the leash from my bag and secure the front end of the gang-line and then unclip tuglines so the dogs can relax. Sumo lifts his leg to one of the icicles. When I unclip Saga, she scratches at a frozen pile of pine needles and then promptly throws herself down. She curls into a ball. They all follow suit, falling like dominoes, all of them curling into tight little balls as soon as I unclip them.

"Thank you," I say to them. "Thank you for trusting me." Then I search behind me. "Guy?"

I struggle back outside. The wind almost blows me back into the cave, but I spy him bent over his dogs. I gesture for Guy to come in.

He hesitates. "I'll tie down the sleds out here. Just bring my dogs inside for me."

"What? There's room in here!" I scream above the howling gusts.

I tug his arm and pull him toward the entrance. Zesty leads the team through the doorway. The solid walls surround us. Again, the relief is immediate.

The stress of being out in the crazy wind and dangerous lake and crashing my sled catches up with me. I begin to tremble. My breathing is ragged and too fast. Guy puts his arm around me.

I shrug him off. "Don't be a dope. I'm not cold."

But my limbs shake uncontrollably. The relief of being out of that incessant wind is enough to make me cry. I bite back the tears. I wouldn't have made it without help. And suddenly I remember. Guy knows about my stupid eyes.

Everything is piling up. I'm going to explode with it. All my emotions are spilling out like Harper's mailbag that burst open.

"We could've died out there," I say, furious at myself for putting my dogs in this situation.

"But you found us a cave." Guy's lips are chapped and raw against his white face.

"Mustard found it." I pull off my scarf with a jerk and shake out the snow.

"Same thing."

Abruptly I notice we're both shivering and probably hypothermic. "We need to build a fire. Have some tea."

This seems to snap Guy out of his daze too. He glances around. "Good idea. The roof is rock so it won't drip on us. We can make a fire there close to the entrance. The smoke can escape. Let me grab some wood from the shore."

I busy myself finding my fire kit and then preparing a spot to light it. The smell of wet dog grounds me. I hear the dogs grumbling to themselves, shaking their heads, their collars jingling. Outside, the wind batters the world.

DECEMBER 29, 1896

DEAR MARGARET,

WE ARRIVED AT THE MICHIPICOTEN POST IN TIME FOR
CHRISTMAS. I AM STILL RECOVERING FROM MY EXPERIENCES,
SO I HAVE BIDDEN FAREWELL TO MY FRIEND MR. MIRON
AND AWAIT THE NEXT COURIER TO COME THROUGH . . .

I HAVE RESIGNED MYSELF TO RAYMOND'S CURE FOR SORE
MUSCLES. HIS SPECIAL RECIPE FOR RUB-ON LINIMENT IS AS
FOLLOWS: ONE PART ALCOHOL, ONE PART TURPENTINE, AND
AN EGG.

YOUR LOVING BROTHER, WILLIAM

CHAPTER 25

Somewhere before Michipicoten,
afternoon of day three

I feed the fire pieces of driftwood, and it crackles with delicious warmth.

My outer mitts are propped up beside it to dry. Our shivering has stopped, but the white patches on Guy's cheeks are still there. I have a touch of frostbite too. The tip of my nose is smarting as it thaws.

Guy stares owlishly at the cave door, muttering something about a portal.

"What's wrong?" I ask.

"It's the portal for the wendigo," Guy says.

"What's a wendigo?"

Guy rubs his face, sheepish. "It's dumb, I know. I grew up hearing how ice caves are doorways to the Otherworld. The malevolent spirit of the early people, the wendigo, was the bringer of winter starvation and disease."

"Stop that! No one is diseased. This portal saved us. You are too much, with your history and weird facts."

"I know. I can't help it. I get obsessed with history sometimes."

"But why?"

He shrugs. "I don't know. It's just something my grandpa got me started on, telling me old stories as he tucked me in when I was a kid. After my mom left, he helped fill the gap. We hung out a lot."

"What do you mean, your mom left? Like, for good?" I immediately dislike his mom.

"I don't see her very often. She's always traveling or . . . off doing some other new thing. She has a lot of interests."

"What about your dad?"

"Yeah, well. I was a hyper kid. Maybe my mom left because I was too much work or something. Maybe my dad thinks that. I don't know. He's never said that," Guy rushes to add when he sees my expression. "Grandpa died last year, and that's when I got super-interested in this race. We've had sled dogs in our family for four generations. I'm running this race to remember my grandpa and keep his stories of my great-great-grandpa alive. Grandpa would've loved this."

I'm not close enough to see his eyes, but I can tell from his voice what they must look like. Full of life.

"What does your dad think about you racing?"

"That's sort of another story. Dad and I have a deal. And it involves me winning this race. Otherwise, he gets rid of the dogs."

"Wait, what?" I can't believe all the deals going on here; the actual dogs running this race would think we're crazy. "Why would he get rid of the dogs?"

"They're expensive is the biggest reason. I've tried to tell him it's our heritage and it's important. But heritage doesn't pay the bills. That's where our deal comes in. Dad has a delivery business. It's not doing so well, so he's talking about selling the dogs. But I looked into it, and you know what? Amazon has started contracting out their package deliveries in Canada. And if my dad wins the Amazon contract for northeastern Ontario, it will save his business. It will be huge. What better way to draw interest to his courier business than for his son to win a dogsled race that celebrates *couriers?* I've got a letter to the department that hires the contractors. It'll be stamped DELIVERED BY DOG TEAM and hopefully grab their attention."

"Oh." I'm too ashamed to say anything else. Dad's porta-potty business has always done well. There's never been a time that I can remember when we worried about money. Dad makes enough so that Mom doesn't need to work. She can keep all her dogs. I can run races. It's never even occurred to me to wonder until now how much it costs to keep a yard of dogs. How have I taken it for granted?

"So if I win, hopefully it gets us noticed, and we win the Amazon contract. Or, at the least, we win the purse, and Dad agrees to keep the dogs. But if I don't win, I'm losing more than the race." He rubs the back of his neck and then says in a smaller voice, "I *need* to win. I have to keep my dogs. Plus, winning would be like celebrating our family."

My heart sinks at his words. If I win, that means Guy doesn't win. "Yeah, that would be amazing," I say.

Guy slaps his thighs so loud the dogs twitch. "Let's talk about something more interesting. Like you."

"I'm not interesting at all."

"Right. So do you have that thing your sister has or what? Stargardt's?"

I pause. A gust of wind roars past the doorway. It feels as if the roar is coming from me. "I don't know for sure. I haven't been diagnosed."

"Well, if you did get diagnosed, maybe you could stop being afraid. You're afraid while you run the dogs, I can tell."

"No, I'm not!"

"You ride the brake all the time."

"What? I do not."

"All. The. Time. And I'll tell you what, that makes no sense since you have more control around corners if you go faster."

"Hello? I've been running dogs since I was born. Can we just agree that we all know how to drive a freaking dog team?"

Neither of us speaks for a moment. The dogs shuffle around. Mustard huffs and grumbles as if he totally agrees with me.

"We all have fears. That's nothing to be ashamed of." Guy points to the Eurohound in his team. "Take Urban over there. He's working out some issues. Like his fear of snakes. And of sticks that look like snakes."

"Listen, I've been living with this a while now, so I don't need you telling me I should stop being afraid and just get tested. It's not that simple."

"Fear of snakes isn't simple either. And imagine how the snakes feel. Really, the only thing that likes a snake is another snake."

I just blink at him.

"What I don't understand," Guy plunges on, "is how you were

able to hide this from your parents. I mean, I've just met you, and *I* can tell."

His words feel like a kick. I shake my head. "I work at being as normal as possible. I've gotten good at pretending. The trick is not to spend much time with them. With anyone. It's just because we're out running dogs that you noticed something wrong."

Guy frowns. "So you avoid spending time with *everyone?*" He looks sad for me. "Well, my point is that *you* know. You can't hide it from yourself, right? So why haven't you told them?"

"The disease progresses differently for everyone. Mine could stay like this, which isn't that bad. I've watched Emma living with Stargardt's. It's torn my parents apart 'cause my mom does everything for her. I don't want her — or anyone — to treat me like that. Like I'm helpless."

He snorts. "Has she met you? You're the least helpless person I know."

A strange hot feeling sinks into me. "If I tell her, she wouldn't let me run dogs. And, I don't know . . . I guess if I don't get tested, I can keep thinking it's not going to affect my life like it has Emma's. It sounds dumb now that I'm saying it out loud."

He touches my knee and says quietly, "It's not dumb."

"Even if it's not, I can't tell my parents. They're too busy dealing with my sister to worry about me."

"So you mean your parents don't *want* to notice. Because they can't be that busy. You're their daughter too. It doesn't make sense what you're saying."

Before I can respond, the dogs all shoot up at once and stare at the opening of the cave.

A shadowy figure stands there. It looks as if it stepped out of the Otherworld. Snow howls in the background, and clouds of snow snake around the figure's legs.

Guy's face drains of color. His mouth opens and closes wordlessly.

"Who's there?" I ask.

The dark figure stumbles into view. "Holy snappin'," she says. "Nice cave!"

January 4, 1897

Dear Margaret,

I now accompany the mail courier Eric Skead who is famous for his record-breaking trip from Pukaskwa Depot to White River, a seventy-mile journey that normally takes four days. He completed it in a mere thirty hours. Such haste was needed when he transported the much-loved foreman Joseph Lefebvre to hospital after he had been severely crushed under a load of pulpwood . . .

Your loving brother, William

CHAPTER 26

Harper!" I grab for her just as she topples over.

She's encrusted in snow. Her lashes are frozen, clinging together with clumps of ice. Her hat is coated with hoarfrost, and her face is haggard and pale; she sort of looks like a frozen chicken. Her dogs are loose, wearing their harnesses and staying close to her like a pack of wolves around a fairy witch.

"Are you okay?"

"Peachy." She wipes her face and looks around. "I am legit freaked out. I mostly just closed my eyes and held on and let the team run. They came right here. Then I saw the glow of your fire."

Over by the wall, Sumo begins growling ominously. A lanky black dog of Harper's stands stiffly, tail flagging up, body erect. The low belly rumble vibrates the ground.

"Grab your dog!" I yell. But it's too late.

Sumo snatches the unlucky dog by its butt. The rest of my team immediately jump to their feet, eager to join in. My dogs. Mongrels. All of them.

Harper's loose dogs hurtle themselves into the fray. And then Guy's team clatters across the cave, dragging the sled over the rocks. We hadn't even staked them out yet. Guy tries to grab the sled to pull them back but can't.

Frenzied snarls echo off the walls. I can't even see Sumo underneath the writhing pile of dogs and teeth and fur.

Horrifying sounds of their fight seep into me and root me where I stand. Mad chaos. Dogs everywhere snapping and scrabbling, some trying to get away, some tearing into whoever appears to be losing. It's the biggest dog brawl I've ever seen.

A shrill "Oh-God-oh-God-oh-God" from Harper finally breaks the spell. I lunge forward.

Harper's black dogs are easy to spot; they're the ones screaming like drama queens. I don't know what they're complaining about. They joined in on purpose. Dogs reflect their owners' personalities, but since Harper hardly runs them, that makes me wonder about her dad.

"Grab him, Guy! That black dog!"

"Yoda! No, Yoda! Listen to me, let go!"

"Harper, get over here! Hold this nutso out of the way! Get that out of your mouth, Damage. Drop it!"

Shrieking, barking, snarling, roaring, yelping, wailing—it fills the ice room. The thick-walled cave amplifies the clamor. We yell at one another to be heard.

I shouldn't be surprised. There are almost twenty dogs in here, stuffed together in a claustrophobic chamber of ice and rock, with all the humans giving off stress vibes. We probably reek of fear. The dogs are just acting it out.

Slowly, Guy and I get a handle on it and haul the dogs apart.

"Grab the stakeout line from my sled!" I shout at Harper. I'm gripping the backs of three of her dogs by their harnesses, the webbing material cutting into my fingers every time they jump.

Finally I heave the last dog off Sumo. And there he is, beaming. One of his ears is decidedly torn and bleeding. I make a tense search through his thick fur, but that appears to be the extent of his injuries. Sumo, at least, is having the time of his life in this cave. Em's dog. He's a lover and a fighter; whatever he's doing, he does it with passion. I just really wish he had more manners doing it.

"You are a bad dog," I tell him as I wipe blood off his neck ruff.

It doesn't stop him from his saucy laughing. He's *laughing*, mouth wide and panting, eyes wild and shining, looking very smug.

"What a ninja-pig party," Guy says.

"Good dog name," I say, and I'm rewarded with a surprised laugh from Guy. "Sorry about that," I say to both of them. "My dogs are all being shipped to Siberia for remedial training in manners after this is over."

January 6, 1897

Dear Margaret,

The mountains were a monumental obstacle. How does one haul a load of three hundred pounds up mountains? Mr. Skead fashioned a pole that he called a broomstick. He sharpened one end of the broomstick and impaled that end into the trail. In this way, the sled wedged against the broomstick while the dogs took a break and did not slip backwards. The broomstick was also helpful while traveling a portion of sideways trail, the pointed end skimming the ground, thereby angling the sled in that direction . . .

Your loving brother, William

CHAPTER 27

O nce all the dogs are staked and under control, we gather around the fire.

I pull out my cooker and make some tea, the familiar motions helping to calm me as well as the dogs. Before I drop my last tea bag into a mug for Harper, I sniff, turn my head aside, press a finger to a nostril and forcefully blow out. I do the other nostril in quick succession. Pouring the water into the mug, I catch Harper's scandalized expression.

"Would you rather have nose-drip in your tea?" I ask.

She presses her lips together, then bursts into a grin. Our fingers touch when I pass her the mug and I feel a connection with her. Even though we're probably the most opposite people ever, I could imagine being friends with Harper if she went to my school.

She shakes her head at me and cackles. "What a dog's breakfast this is."

"What were you doing out there?" Guy asks Harper. "Why even come out on the lake? You must've seen the blow before you left the trees, since you were behind us."

"I had to. I have to win. Didn't she tell you?" She nods at me. "Dad's got a lot riding on this race. He just needs this win to finish off his season, and he'll beat out Mandy Carmichael for top musher and the Energence Dog Food sponsorship. He thought having me in the race would give us more media coverage. And if I win, I *never* have to race another one. I'm winning this thing if it kills me."

"Well, how are you going to do that when I'm winning this thing?" Guy says.

He meant it to be teasing. We all see he's got only five dogs left compared to Harper's six faster dogs. He had to drop Captain Jack at the last checkpoint with the same stomach bug that Icon had. But his comment comes out sounding a bit desperate and strained. The words are left to hang there.

All three of us sit around the fire and eye one another as we sip our tea.

Each of us needs to win.

I squeeze my mug as I realize we're the top teams now. The

three youngest mushers in the race. Bondar and Gant are still somewhere behind us. Unless they've passed us in the storm, which isn't very likely.

"Everyone has probably had to find a place to hide from the storm, right?" Harper echoes my thoughts. "So I think that means we're ahead. Hard to know until all the times get added, but if we're faster on this leg, that would even things out."

"Yup," Guy says.

The tension in the cave is rising. If only all of us could win. I want Harper to win so she can gain her freedom. I want Guy to keep his dogs and carry his family legacy. And I want to be able to save my independence before my world gets turned upside down.

Who am I kidding? I couldn't have gotten across that last bay without help. I can't even deliver the *mail*.

My missing mailbag ignites a burning hole in my gut every time I think of it. Now that Em is going to tell my secret, I really cannot lose this race. But how can I possibly win?

"This reminds me of one of William Desjardins's adventures," Guy says.

I groan inwardly. The last thing I need to hear right now is another letter about heroic mail couriers when I've failed so spectacularly with my own attempt.

"Who is William Desjardins?" Harper says.

"I'm glad you asked," Guy says, pulling out his book. "I bet you didn't know I have a famous great-great-gramps. I think we're stuck here for a bit, so who wants to hear a story?"

Harper shrugs and blows on her tea.

Guy begins reading. As we listen, I lean over and add another piece of driftwood to the fire. It sparks and snaps and blasts my face with heat. The wind moans outside.

"Okay, wait." Harper interrupts Guy, holding a finger up. "You said it takes four *days* to get to White River from here?"

"Four days for them," Guy says. "It's seventy miles, so about a day for us. They carried more, their dogs were bigger, and I don't imagine their trails were as nice."

Harper mutters under her breath, something about crazy mail couriers needing to get a life. Guy continues reading, ignoring her, until she interrupts again. "They used that sharpened stick like a gee pole to help control the sled? The mountains are that steep?"

"Sounds like it," Guy says.

"Awesome. So you read about this stuff in your spare time, or is this for a school project or something?" Harper asks.

"Don't you find it interesting, especially since we're running this race? Imagine delivering that mail that you're carrying a hundred years ago."

"I'm imagining myself . . . yes . . . yes, I see it." Harper closes her eyes and theatrically waves a hand. "Yes, I see myself carrying *many* bags. I'm shopping with all of my winnings. You're right, this *is* an interesting game!"

I burst out laughing. Harper and I share a chuckle while Guy pretends to be offended.

After that, a silence settles. We're all lost in our own thoughts. Gusts blow past the cave opening, and some sneak their way inside. They shove the sparks around. Smoke stings my eyes.

The smoke mingles with the smell of wet dog and our thawing mitts and gloves. It's become warm in here, but I don't dare remove my hat. I know my hair is a rat's nest caked with dried sweat and grease from an appalling lack of showers. My hands are wrapped around my cooling mug. They ache from all the time spent freezing while checking dogs. They're chapped and covered in nicks and scrapes and dried blood, and there's dirt caked around my fingernails.

I realize I'm exhausted. It's been three days now of working on very little sleep. I'm running on fumes. I've been so busy making sure the dogs are taken care of and fed and healthy and getting their rest, I haven't spent a lot of time keeping myself healthy.

My eyelids are heavy. I snuggle farther into my sleeping bag and put my cup down so I don't wear the tea. I see Guy's and Harper's heads nodding too. Everyone is so tired.

"I wonder how long this will blow?" Harper says. "We're stuck here for a while, it looks like. No one is moving in this." Then she curls up with her back to me.

Guy does the same. I watch the flames burn lower until I close my eyes for a moment to rest them. The last thing I hear is Mustard talking in his sleep.

"McKenna! Get up!" Guy is bending over me, shaking me awake.

I bolt upright so fast I get dizzy. "What?"

"Harper made a break for it while we slept."

"Wh-what?" I search around for Harper. Guy is right. She's no longer lying in her sleeping bag by the fire. Her sleeping bag is gone.

Her dogs are gone.

CHAPTER 28

Harper has given us the classic slip.

"Come on," Guy says. "We have to go catch her! She must've just been pretending to sleep and now she's gone ahead to win. Gah! I can't believe I fell for that! Oldest trick in the book. How far ahead do you think she is?"

We both look outside. The wind is still blowing the snow sideways, though it doesn't seem as violent. I think it's calming down, but now it's darker out so I won't be able to see well.

I check my watch, not bothering to hide how close I bring it to my face. It's half past four in the afternoon. "We slept for over an hour," I say.

"How could she have left without waking us up?" Guy asks.

"She's trying to win. Us staying here is part of the play. Why would she wake us up?" I start packing my cooker and mugs.

"I mean, *how* did she do it? You didn't hear her at all?" Guy stuffs his sleeping bag in his sled. He shrugs on his down jacket and his anorak.

"Wait. Just wait. You're actually going out in the wind? Do you remember what it was like out there?" I'm getting anxious now as the reality sets in. Harper is going to win this race if we don't leave right now. But the last thing I want to do is go out in that wind again. I can't believe how crazy that girl is. But really, she doesn't know any better. She doesn't have the experience Guy and I have to even know what dangers are out there. The fact she's gotten by this far is a combination of sheer luck, some physical skills, and her amazing dogs. But still, it takes courage to keep going. I shake my head with reluctant admiration. She's got grit.

"The wind's slowed down. It's not as bad as before," Guys says. "I'll be your guide musher."

"My what?"

"That woman who ran the Iditarod, she was blind but they let her race if she used a guide musher."

"Who? A blind musher? Like, how blind? Did she have Stargardt's?"

"I don't know. I don't think so. I'd never heard of it before I met you."

I'm trying to process this information. Why haven't I heard

of this musher running the Iditarod? But as the snow whips by outside, I have to focus. "I don't need a guide team. I'm not blind."

Guy makes a frustrated growl and turns to face me. "Hey, I think you're amazing. Obviously. I know you can do it. But what did you say about aids and how if your sister uses aids, it evens the playing field? Isn't that what I'd be, just another aid? You still have to handle your own sled. It's not like I'm suggesting I'll run the race for you."

I know I'm acting like an idiot. And what he's saying makes sense. I take a deep breath. "So, how did she use a guide musher? Like a team that ran in front of her dogs the whole way?"

"They used earpieces, I think, to communicate. The guide let her know when corners were coming, I guess. I didn't pay attention to most of it, just how it related to Zesty. I thought it was cool. The point is, I can run in lead, and we can get back in the race! Come on!"

I glance at the dogs. They're all still curled up, but their eyes are trained on me. They know an opportunity when they see it. I nod.

"And how did you guys let Harper and her dogs leave without telling me?" I demand as I make my way to the sled. Mustard gets up slowly and performs a long luxurious downward-dog stretch. That appears to be the cue for everyone else to uncurl, stand, and stretch. Tails wagging. Seems they think this is a fine idea. Surprising, since they didn't seem so keen the last time we were out there.

"Don't you guys see the wind? Are you sure?"

Arooooooooo, Mustard says, and then sneezes with feeling.

It doesn't take us but a few minutes to pack up our makeshift camp. I don't think too far ahead, but once the sleds are ready and the dogs are ready and we're heading out, my heart begins to pound.

The wind wallops us as soon as we step outside. It *has* slowed down, but it's still blowing snow particles so hard, they feel like little knives hitting my face. The wind sucks away my gasp of dismay. *Are we really doing this?*

Maybe Harper doesn't know any better, but we do. If we get into trouble out here, it will be our own fault. We're going into this with our eyes wide open to the risks. But something I've learned running dogs: the joy you get from doing something isn't as intense if there isn't any risk.

Guy gives me the thumbs-up and pulls his hook. "Ready? Let's go catch her."

As soon as we get past the cliffs, the full wind hits us.

The trail leads straight out across the bay and into the dusk.

My sled bag acts like a sail, catching the wind. I struggle to keep the sled from tipping over in the gusts.

Once we cross the bay, the trees will give us some protection from the wind. It will be okay once we get into the trees. But twilight is descending fast all around us. Not only is it a race to catch up to Harper, it's a race to get off the bay before the cloak of night falls.

On our left, something dark moves across the ice. And then past us.

"Driftwood!" Guy yells above the wind. "Heads up!"

All I see are dark shapes and more dark shapes flying past us. Where is all this driftwood coming from?

The wind claws down my throat. Guy gee-haws Zesty and Diesel around the driftwood. I hear his commands over the wind and see his team doing a graceful ballet across the ice.

Guy's voice is guiding Zesty. When he yells, *"Gee-gee-gee,"* that means we have to make a hard right. When he says it softer and slower, it means we have to make a gentler arcing right turn.

When I tell non-mushers about how I steer the dogs, they seem to think it's like driving a car. As if I can step on the accelerator when I want more speed or make them turn left or right, as if I'm driving between traffic cones.

I've tried to explain. "They're dogs with real personalities and fears and wants and needs. They are not a car."

But Zesty is weaving between the blowing driftwood like a well-tuned machine. She and Guy are a team. Even though she can't see, Zesty is sensing what Guy wants, how much she should turn. It's as though they're sharing one mind. Guy is her eyes. Just like Mustard is mine.

I don't know many dogs who could lead in this right now. Zesty, along with Diesel, is leading both of our teams. She's a blind dog doing the work of a regular sled dog. An *exceptional* sled dog. Guy was right.

A thought hits me so hard, I physically feel the impact at my core. It's something I've known all along but haven't really understood until this moment. A jolt of comprehension shifts my world.

Zesty is not disabled. Her differences make her better.

CHAPTER 29

O nce we finally leave the lake ice, the furious wind is buffered by the trees.

It's a straight run on flat trails under a dark blanket of night. The cool thing about running this race along the north shore of Lake Superior is the dense woods. That deep sense of quiet and solitude that I love so much on the trail at home is even more pronounced here. There are longer stretches where you don't find any civilization. We run for hours without seeing another soul. No cities or towns or houses or people or traffic. Not even a plane going by. It's like the end of the earth out here. It makes you feel as if you're the only person alive.

The Canadian wilderness is immense and stark and dangerous and beautiful. And it hasn't changed much since the couriers went through here. The land is the same—indifferent to all who travel along its trails.

Ahead I see the flash of a headlamp wink at me and I smile. It's nice not to be *completely* alone. I respond with my own flash and then turn it off again. The dogs don't need the light to see. They smell the trail easy enough.

We run and run. The dogs are tireless. They continually amaze me with what they can do. But we don't catch up to Harper. Not that I'd imagined we would with those dogs of hers. Still, we had to try. And since everything is timed, our run tonight will count for something.

I check on my dogs with my headlamp, aiming it along the team. I have the light off center, not right on my forehead but on the side, so I can turn my head to study each dog in my periphery. Even with the trees to block it, the wind gusts are blowing snow around. My light catches particles in its beam and reflects back. Diamonds of light glitter in the air and streak past me like I'm in a video game.

Through it, I can still see my dogs. Everyone has tight tugs. Everyone is trotting, tail straight, ears forward. Even Aspen looks good, no sign of soreness or slowing down. In fact, the dogs seem faster and stronger than when we started this race. They thrive on the exercise and the new smells and scenery. They're all working like a single unit, matching their pace, intent on enjoying the smooth night trail.

I hold them back with the drag. We'd be going faster if we were alone, not behind a team with only five dogs. But I'm grateful to Guy for helping us across the bay, so I keep my dogs back.

Eventually, the lights of the Pukaskwa checkpoint glow through the trees ahead. We didn't catch up to Harper. But there's still one more section to run after this. We haven't lost yet. Harper has to stay at the checkpoint for her mandatory six-hour layover before heading back out. It will give us a chance to catch up.

We sign in with the officials and their clipboards and stopwatches. "When did Harper Bowers come through?" I ask.

"Looks like twenty-three minutes ago," he says, studying the board.

"What about Bondar? Gant?"

"Not yet. You're the only teams arrived in this storm. You crazy juniors are leading the race."

I peer around, looking for my family and my dog truck. This checkpoint is just a hastily erected shelter tent in the middle of nowhere. There's a landing area where a few dog trucks are waiting. Floodlights are on around the tent. There aren't any handlers out here by the trail.

"Where is everyone?" I ask. "Where are all the trucks?"

"Only some got through before they closed the highway. There's a blizzard going on, in case you missed it. And with the winds, there's zero visibility on the roads."

I sink my hook, drop to the ground, and crawl through the team to thank the dogs. I kneel next to Mustard and we share a deep discussion about lost mail and secret deals and lost freedom. "But I understand what I have to do now, Mustard," I say. "I have a new plan."

Aroooo. He peers back at me with knowing eyes. There's ice coating each of his long chin hairs. The floodlights nearby make the whiskers glow.

The sound of snow crunching behind me makes me sit up and turn. Harper is standing next to me. "Did you see the driftwood?" she asks. Her voice comes out high and tight. Terrorized.

"Yeah, we saw the driftwood. Thanks for that." We wouldn't have been out there to see it if we weren't chasing her.

"Well, I saw one piece a bit too close. It crashed into my sled and freaked me out so much that I've scratched."

It takes several seconds for this to sink in. "You what? You . . . what?" My mind is sluggish.

"Yup. And I have you to thank. If I hadn't finally told my dad after the first day like you suggested, he'd probably make me keep going. But when I came in tonight, he'd been so scared for me and felt bad for pushing. He said no sponsorship is worth my safety. And he said he believed I was going to change my mind and realize how great dogsledding is. Like that's going to happen in a blizzard. So guess what — we're going home."

"But . . . you're winning. And you have only one more section. There's sixty miles left in the race."

"Yeah, but it's the Cascades. I've been dreading them since the start. I just can't do it."

A fresh stab of fear hits me. Right. How could I forget?

"So I just have to turn in my mailbag," Harper is saying, "plus this other mailbag I found on the trail."

Suddenly, I can't quite breathe. "What other mailbag?"

"Yeah, it was lying on the trail, and I just scooped it up as we went by. Some loser is going to be surprised when they get to the finish and can't find their mail!"

"Can you show me?"

In a daze, I follow her to her sled next to her dog truck. Her dad is feeding the dogs. I suppose that's allowed now that she's scratched. When she hands me the mailbag, my knees almost buckle. "This is mine."

"Really?" She grins at me. "Now we're even again, huh?"

I lunge and wrap my arms around her. She laughs in surprise and hugs me back. She smells, oddly, like strawberries. How is that even possible after three days on the trail?

Relief flows through my limbs. I clutch the bag to my chest. As I make my way back to my dogs, I also realize nothing has changed. I'm still going to go through with my plan. The one I worked out on the lake after watching Zesty. But the knot that had formed in my gut over worrying about the mail is gone.

A short while later, the dog trucks arrive. I guess the highway reopened. But still no other teams have come in, so that's good news. I stand and wait for my family to find me.

"McKenna!" Mom's voice.

Three figures come toward me. Once they're closer I can tell by their shape who is who, but it's so dark out here, I can't see their expressions. Mom grabs me, holds me out at arm's length, then pulls me close. Em wraps her arms around my hips with a strength that conveys how worried she'd been.

"How did you run through this storm?" Dad asks.

"I had some good friends," I say. "There's something I have to tell you guys."

January 26, 1897

Dear William,

I do not know when you might receive this dreadful news; we have not heard from you in over a fortnight. I am sorry to tell you our dear young Anna has been stricken with the awful ravages of cholera. She has succumbed. The loss is unbearable. We are overwrought with grief. Please come home immediately.

Your sister, Margaret

CHAPTER 30

Pukaskwa checkpoint
60 miles to finish

W hat is it?" Mom asks.

We're all seated at a folding table inside the shelter tent. Nervous energy skates down my legs. My right knee won't stop jerking.

"What do you need to tell us?"

I look at them fully, with my head angled a little off to the side so I can see their expressions. I've been careful not to look at them this way for so long, and it feels good to finally see them completely.

"For a while now," I begin, "I've had issues with my vision."

"*What?*" Mom pales. Stands up.

"What kind of issues?" Dad says at the same time.

Emma bites her lip.

I feel impaled by spears of ice, but I keep going. "I wasn't sure for a long time, that's why I didn't tell you. But just before the race started, I realized that I have Stargardt disease." My voice trembles.

"But how do you know? Could it be you just need glasses?" Dad asks. "That might be all it is."

We look at each other and pause. Time seems to slow down. I watch him study my face for the truth. I watch his emotions go from disbelief to uncertainty. From denial to defeat. I see the realization come over him that both of his daughters have this. I can tell the exact moment when it hits him. And it breaks me.

It sweeps across his face, raw and real. His shoulders slump, his eyes turn red, he covers his head with his hands and folds in on himself. He begins to cry in deep gasping sobs.

In all of the hundreds of scenarios of this moment I've envisioned, I had never considered my father reacting this way. I've always imagined how it would destroy my mom. Somehow, I hadn't even been worried about my dad.

I stare at him in shock. I've never seen my dad cry, not even when we got the news about Emma. It scares me so badly that for a moment I'm frozen. Then my throat closes up.

This is happening so fast. We've only just started talking about it. It's as if Dad already suspected . . . I finally realize something that I should have seen sooner. *Dad has known all along.* It was his fear that kept him from accepting it.

It's such a strange new thing for me to suddenly see him as a human rather than just my dad.

Em's hand snakes into mine. Mom seems shocked. She's motionless for a breath, her face worn and heartbroken. And then she reaches a hand to Dad's back. His shoulders shake and terrible strangled noises come out of him. He sounds like an animal in pain. I put my other hand on his knee. Dad reaches for me abruptly. He stands and pulls me up with him and wraps me in a bear hug. Then Emma squeezes in and Mom joins us.

All four of us huddle together in our own bubble of grief.

The dogs needed tending to. I'm still in a race, after all. That was a good excuse to take some time away and collect my thoughts. By now we've all recovered a bit from the news bomb.

Mom crunches over to me while I'm massaging Aspen. She's carrying Em and sets her down. It galls me that she's still doing that.

"What I don't understand is how," Mom says. "It's not fair both of you are affected. How could one family be so unlucky?"

Anger flares up. "Mom. So we've got low vision. Whoop-de-do. There are worse things in life! We spend so much time worrying about what Em can't do anymore when we should be thinking about what she *can* do. What *I* can do. And what a blind lead dog can do."

"What?"

"We'll have to talk about this more later. But for now, I just wanted you guys to know before I finished the race."

"If you think you're finishing this race, you are sadly mistaken, young lady," Mom says. She tries to sound stern, but I hear what she's saying underneath her words. She's so afraid for me.

"Mom. I can do this. Look at how far I've come! And nothing has changed with my vision from when I first started. I've done almost the whole race like this and done well. I've more than done well. I'm winning, now that Harper has scratched."

I spare a thought for Guy, the other team ahead with me, but I don't dwell on it.

"I could win! And don't forget, I promised I'd deliver the letters from Em's class. Her whole class is counting on me. I *am* going to finish this."

"Beth," Dad says softly. He reaches for her hand. "Remember what the doctor said when you asked about donating an eye?"

My head shoots up. "What?" *She tried to give Emma her own eye?*

"Sometimes, there is nothing we can do to help them," Dad continues, speaking to Mom. "She needs to finish."

I turn to him. "I'm not pretending anymore. It *is* harder for me now. It doesn't do any good to ignore that I have a vision impairment. Em and I both. And it's not going to go away. We have to learn to live with it. We all have to learn. I think we need to go back to the counselor from the Blind Institute. We need help accepting this and learning how to live with it. Like in Em's case, if she needs to use a cane, then she should learn how."

"I just don't think it's safe for you," Mom says. "You have to face that there are things you can't do."

"No," I say. "And I'm going to prove it."

I put a hand on Emma's shoulder so she knows I'm talking directly to her. "Yes, we've got low vision. And that's okay. We can still do what everyone else does. We just do it differently."

Emma nods fiercely. "Go deliver my letter—"

She's interrupted by the sound of a team coming. The musher arrives at the checkpoint, and the timers race over to sign him in. When I hear his voice, my heart sinks. It's Bondar. He isn't that far behind after all.

January 28, 1897

Dearest Anna,

I have been too busy to write since arriving in White
River. I wanted to tell you about traveling here
from Michipicoten. The beauty of the mountains,
narrow gorges, and flat frozen bogs struck us. The
dogs, being five and seventy pounds to ninety pounds
each, together can pull more than Charlie! Now I
will stay here until next summer . . .

Regarding your wish to be an adventurer; I heard
of a lady, Anna Jameson, who traveled with the
voyageurs in the canoes! So I believe you can grow
up to be whoever you want to be, regardless of your
fair gender.

Love, Uncle William

CHAPTER 31

As soon as our mandatory six hours of rest was over, both Guy and I set out from the Pukaskwa checkpoint together on the final run.

That meant we started at two a.m., so it's been several hours in the dark. But now the creeping morning light is illuminating the sky and brightening the trail. This weird warm weather has made the going hard. The dogs are cranky. I'd taken off their booties to keep them cooler, using wax instead to protect their feet. But they're still hot.

Everything is soggy and slushy, and the trail is punchy and soft. After all the crazy wind, the air is finally still. The wind must've blown in this warm front. But the biggest problem, according to Guy, is the blanket of fog.

"I can't see a thing in this soup," he complains once we've pulled over to give the dogs a chance to cool off. "I can barely see past my leaders."

We're in a stand of jack pine, judging from the smell in the air. They give off a distinct pine-pitchy odor. "I can barely see past my leaders every day. This is normal for me." I notice that there's fog in my peripheral vision, but it doesn't bother me as much as it does him.

A thought hits me. I give him a smug grin. "Don't worry, Guy. I can be your guide team. You need an aid to get through this fog."

He gives me a slow smile.

"If I can't see what's up ahead, I can't warn Zesty," he says. "But your leaders can see for themselves. I think it's a good idea. Just till we get through this fog. After that, it's back to racing, right?"

I call up the dogs. "Agreed. Let's go, Mustard. On by."

The dogs on both teams give one another good sniffs as they slowly pass on the narrow trail. They obviously remember the brawl, but that doesn't seem to faze them in the slightest. All is forgiven.

My mind reaches ahead to the problem of the day. The Cascades are up there somewhere. It's become this larger-than-life thing, with the anticipation building these last four days. A shadow waiting in a corner of my thoughts. And now it's finally here, about to be unveiled. I can at last see what I'm dealing with.

We plod around a bend and trek our way over some rolling hills. The dogs continually punch through the top crust of the trail. Our speed is reduced to a crawl. I struggle in the soupy mess just like them, trying to jog next to the sled. I keep tripping, sliding, falling, grabbing hold of the handlebar to pull myself up again. It's like running in a bowl of oatmeal. Steam rises off my head when I take my hat off. Sweat runs into my eyes. I shed my anorak, and steam billows off my fleece jacket.

Damp, sodden, listless weather. The trees appear soaked, black and wet. All around us in the woods, I hear the dripping of snow melting off branches. The runners make a wet hiss over the trail. Each time I lift a foot, my boot is heavy with sticky snow.

We slip down one last little hill and then we begin to climb. On our left is a jagged rock wall decorated with glistening wet icicles and clinging green moss. The trail follows it upward.

The chore of climbing is made even harder by how slow we're going. I constantly have to wrestle with the sled. Guy was right. The slower you run, the harder it is to make the sled go where you want. My brush bow keeps banging into trees. I have to haul it off the tree and then shove it back onto the trail.

Sumo struggles through the heavy snow. He's going to over-heat for sure today. I'm so impressed he's made it almost the entire race. I feel a sense of pride as I realize that all of my dogs are going to get to the finish line now, even if I have to carry them in the basket. I will have finished this race without dropping a single one of them. I can't wait to point that out to Mom. I don't think she's ever accomplished a race like this without a dropped dog.

On the trail, Lizard and Damage slip but right themselves again. Then Sumo and Haze go down. I brace for it. The sled skids sideways on a patch of ice that lies hidden under a thin layer of snow. Once we're across, the sled gains traction on the solid trail again.

"Watch out!" I yell back to Guy. "I think we're coming to the start of the Cascades."

On my left, the rockface we're running beside disappears up into the fog. On my right, the cliff drops off. I cannot see how far down it falls. We're kissing the edge of it. I hear water running.

Mustard slips. Claws. Gets back on the trail. I angle to the left and dig the heel of my boot off the runner for grip. It helps to steer the sled over.

We slip and skate over the ice that's formed across the trail. It slopes to the right and then drops away. There's just a chasm of air beyond my right runner. How far does it drop?

Don't think about it. I focus on the trail and where we are right now.

The trail narrows as it hugs the rim. We're still climbing, struggling slowly up. The icy section ends, and once more we're on solid snow. Are we through? Is that it? After all the buildup. After everyone talking about this deadly spot for the entire race, it feels almost anticlimactic that I didn't crash.

No sooner have I let myself believe I've done it than I feel the sled slip again. "Another patch here!" I call over my shoulder.

I haul on the handlebar, pulling it to the left to steer the sled. When the sled starts to skid, I lean far out over the left runner to pull the right runner up in the air, like I'm popping a wheelie. The left ski bites into the ice like an ice skate. I balance the sled on its edge as if I'm leaning out on a small sailboat with my pontoon skimming the water. The trick to heeling on the fine edge is not to let yourself get too far over either side.

We cross the ice. I let the sled down. We hit another patch. I tip it up. Each time, I yell a warning out to Guy.

I can tell when another patch of ice is coming by the dogs' reaction. Plus, I can sense it. I don't know how; my body just instinctively reacts to how the sled feels, the slight change in pitch from the runners. It's exhausting and exhilarating and consumes my whole world at this moment.

We crest the mountain and then the trail begins to descend. The angle is steeper going down than it was coming up. It seems Harvey was right. It's one long run down.

We skitter and clatter, building speed. I jump on and off the runners, angling, tilting, manhandling the sled. My arms burn from the exertion and tension. I'm glad it requires my full concentration. I don't have time to freak out.

We hit another patch of ice. This one is different. It continues on. We skid for several car lengths across. And still it continues. All exposed ice. Panic crashes through my chest. *This is bad.*

Has the trail crew even been through here to look at this? With the warm weather, the ice has become ridiculous. The melt from the mountain drips and then freezes again once the air cools. The freeze and thaw with the weather this season created that perfect ice cave that sheltered us. And it created more and more ice on this trail. It's now a full-on hazard, a slanted luge of death. How do they expect us to run dogs across this? It wouldn't be so bad if it were flat, but with the angle, it's insane.

We're almost across. The dogs tiptoe, using their claws to stay on the slick trail. My arms shake. My blood throbs with the effort. I can't quite maintain balance the whole way. We touch down. Immediately the sled begins to slide. Once it starts, we slide faster.

I can't stop. We barrel toward the edge. The sled's going to pull all the dogs with it.

Sumo takes the weight of my free fall first. He slams into his harness.

"Up, up, Sumo!" I yell, desperate. "Come on, boy!"

He digs in. Leaning into it, he pulls with all his heart. The weight of the sled and my weight combined should be tugging him sideways, should be pulling us all down into the gorge. But Sumo somehow keeps the sled on course. He strains. He puts his head down and steamrolls forward.

I've never been more glad about bringing a dog in my life. "Good boy, Sumo!" If not for him, the sled would be sliding off this mountain, dragging the smaller dogs with it.

In my total focus, the end of the ice comes as a surprise. We glide to a stop on the solid snow of the trail. All the dogs immediately dive into the snow to take bites of it and cool their bellies.

I sink to my knees beside them in relief and bury my face in Sumo's ruff. "Good job! What a team!"

I turn to see how Guy is doing. "It ends here!" I shout.

That's when I hear the yell. And then a horrible smashing noise.

CHAPTER 32

I can't see anything behind me, just a wall of fog.

With impatience, I tie my snub line to a tree and tell my team, "Wait here!"

Frantically, I shuffle out over the ice patch and cup my hands around my mouth. "Guy? Where are you?"

I hear the panting before I see them. Out of the fog, Guy's dogs scramble toward me. I let out a breath in relief.

But then the sled appears and there is no Guy.

Zesty plows into me, adjusts her course, and continues past. I line up to catch the sled. Wheel dogs bearing down. Heartbeats count the seconds. *Thud. Thud. Thud.*

Lunge!

I reach for the handlebar. It collapses under my weight. Both of the upright stanchions are busted and just hanging by the

Velcro straps of the sled bag. I topple on top of it. Once the dogs hit the solid trail, they take off.

I clutch the brake bar, bouncing on my stomach behind the broken sled. But all my time spent wiping out this season pays off. By now, I'm an expert at getting dragged. I reach out and sink the hook like I've done a million times. The team stops.

I lie there, gasping for air. *No time!* I haul myself up.

Quickly, I secure the sled and then race back toward the Cascades. My feet slip and slide in the mushy trail. My team is still happily lounging. Mustard has his feet crossed over each other as if he's sunbathing on vacation.

"Stay here," I say with a wheeze as I run by. Still no sign of Guy.

I creep over to the edge of the ice where it drops off the trail. "Guy? Guy! Where are you? I can't see you, so you have to answer back!"

"McKenna!" he yells from not too far below me. "My team!"

Relief floods through me. "Yes, I caught them. Are you okay?"

"You wouldn't happen to have any eggs and turpentine would you?"

Something between a laugh and a cry escapes me. Yup, he's good. Still weird. "Can you get your sore muscles back up here?"

"I might need a hand."

Slowly, guided by the sound of his voice, I find him. There's nothing to grab hold of on the ice. I'm clinging to it by my fingernails. It's like thick yellowish varnish over the whole trail, superslick. How am I going to help Guy up?

"Hang on," I say, and I scrabble back to my sled. I find my ax and then, panting hard, skid back to the spot on the ice where Guy fell off. If I'm not careful, I'll slip right off too, and then we'll both be stuck. I whack the ax blade into the trail, then hang on to the handle with one hand and extend my other hand down.

"Can you reach?" I ask. I feel his fingers touching the tips of mine.

"Come closer," he says.

I slide my grip down the ax handle as far as I dare. It gets me another inch lower. Guy grasps my hand. He pulls. It's as though I'm on a torture rack, both arms stretched wide.

"Ungh!" Somehow, I hold on while my arm is practically pulled out of its socket.

"Faster," I say as my grip begins to slip down the handle. "Little faster, please!"

Guy grunts and climbs until, at last, he appears beside me. We crawl off the ice and over to where my dogs wait. And then we collapse onto the snow. I roll over onto my back, blood thundering in my ears.

"Good thing you're blind or you'd have seen me pee my pants back there."

My arm flops over to smack him. "Good thing I'm strong, you mean. What do you weigh, like three hundred pounds?"

"You'd make a good mail courier too. Stubborn like bull. Smart like fox."

We both sit up abruptly, as if remembering at the same time we're in a race. Guy jogs over to check his team. I hear his dismay. "Oh no! My sled!"

I join him. "We can repair it. The basket is still solid."

Guy glances past me down the trail we just came from. "There's no time for that! We don't know how much of a lead we have. But I can't use it like this; there's nothing to hold on to."

We're silent as Guy tries fitting the stanchions back together. I see what he means. There's no way he can use this sled. And making new stanchions would take too long.

"You could join your dogs with mine," I suggest. "One long gangline. We'll run in together."

"Then we'll both be disqualified," Guy points out. "Neither of us will win."

I look over at my sled. I'm close to winning this race, to proving what a sight-impaired person can do. How satisfying would that be?

Guy is close to winning too. And thanks to Harper, I've got my mailbag back. I can deliver Emma's letter.

But Guy needs to keep his dogs.

"Use mine." The words come suddenly, surprising me. But I mean them.

"What? No, I can't leave you here."

"Guy, you could win this whole race if you go now! Go — win the race, keep your dogs. Go deliver the mail! Isn't that what you came for? Think of your grandpa."

Guy searches my face. "But you should win this race. You've got more dogs than me. You're a faster, stronger team."

We look at each other as precious seconds tick by. We have no more time to discuss this. "I know I could win. That's enough for me. Now go."

Guy looks over at my sled, then back at his small team. "I could go and then come right back for you. We're only what, about ten miles from the finish? I could be back soon. Are you sure?"

"Just hurry. We've no idea where Bondar is."

CHAPTER 33

10 miles from the finish line

While I wait, I sit with Mustard in the snow and stroke his forehead.

"Sorry, bud," I say. "I know you wanted to win."

He rests his chin on my leg, stares up at me. I'm overcome with love for him. I'm lucky to be able to run these dogs. And I think Mustard's been trying to tell me that. It's so easy to focus on the things that we don't have rather than the things that we do have.

Mustard snorts.

"You'll get over it," I say.

Inside of me, I have warring feelings. To be honest, I'm a bit deflated I won't get to cross the finish line on my own. After all the work to get here, I'd love to complete the race as a whole team —just me and my awesome dogs.

But that doesn't quite beat the warm feeling of satisfaction I have knowing Guy will win this race. He's going to keep his dogs. I smile.

The noise of something approaching breaks through my thoughts. I hear sliding on ice, runners clattering. Someone swearing. Dogs panting. And then out of the fog, Marc Bondar comes through. He glances at me. "You okay?"

"Oh, yeah. Someone's coming to get me. Don't worry."

As he runs by and continues on down the trail, I check my watch. He's only a few minutes behind Guy.

I stand, full of nervous energy now. My dogs are offended by Bondar passing. They're up too and whining. Sumo pegs me with a look that would be comical if I didn't fully understand him. *How long are we going to have to wait here?*

I glance at Guy's broken sled. It's just sitting there on the side of the trail looking forlorn and lopsided. The broken stanchions jut out from the back of the sled. With the front of the sled angled upward, it looks like a drunken grin.

I shuffle over to the stanchions and wiggle them. They're cracked all the way up the length of wood. When I flex them, they break apart into shorter pieces. *Wow, Guy. How hard did you roll this thing?*

I fold the bottoms of the stanchions inward onto the sled floor and tuck the pieces that broke off into the sled bag. Some of Guy's gear is still inside the sled bag. He hadn't grabbed it when he took mine. Gingerly, I move the gear and sit on the sled. I bounce slightly.

Could I . . .

I inspect the bridle where the gangline gets attached. It's solid when I tug on it. Nothing seems broken except the stanchions. The only thing wrong with the sled is there is nothing for a musher to hold on to and steer with.

What if I just laid down on top of it like I was riding a toboggan and hung on? It sounded like that's how Harper ran the race —just closing her eyes, hanging on to the back of her sled. And somehow, she got through some pretty crazy sections.

I check out my full team of eight strong and manic dogs. I peer up ahead at the trail. It's only about ten miles. What could go wrong?

I grin.

Suddenly, I'm in a hurry. I want to catch up with Bondar. My dogs obviously do too. They're full of zip.

"We're doing this," I tell them.

It doesn't take long to hook the carabiners on the gangline into the bridle of the sled. I screw them closed, reattach tuglines, and then hop on the toboggan. My weight shifts the bag around on the smooth bed of plastic underneath. It's a weird angle from down here. I can't see as far. But then again, I can't see far lately anyway. Without overthinking, I reach out and pull the hook.

"Ready? All right!" The dogs take a second to realize that they get to run again. There's something different going on back at the sled. They glance behind them, and then, as if shrugging it off, turn back to the trail, and the sled takes off like a jet.

Immediately I realize that this is going to be wild.

I slide on the narrow bed as soon as we start down the trail. Every bump threatens to throw me off. I cling to the sides of the toboggan. The dogs dart around the first corner and the sled keeps going straight, then jerks to follow them. I almost go flying. Without the handlebar and since I'm not able to bend and lean, there is no steering. And the brake is behind me. I can't reach back and shove it down without losing my tenuous grip on the sled.

Snow and ice pellets spray me on the face while I try to think.

Suddenly, I remember the gee pole that the old couriers used to control their sleds in Guy's story. We barrel around another corner, and I just barely avoid somersaulting off. As we careen down the trail, I cling to the toboggan with one hand and root around underneath me with the other. When I feel the broken stanchion pieces, I pull them out. They're pointy and jagged on the ends.

I grip one in each hand and use them to dig into the trail. It keeps me centered on the toboggan bed. I shove the right one down and the sled pulls over to the right. I dig the other one into the trail, and it brings the sled over the other way. I can use these to steer. I whoop out loud.

"*Yip, yip, yip!* Let's get to that finish line, guys!"

In the end, I was right about the ride being wild.

By the time we cross the line and the timers stop their watches, I'm coated all over with hoarfrost. I'd lost my hat way back on the trail. My ears are burning and feel like ice cubes. My hair is full of snow and sticking up. My eyes and nose stream goo, which has frozen on my face. And I'm certain my wide grin makes me look like a lunatic. But I can't stop smiling.

There's a crowd gathered, probably because Guy and Bondar had come through. So I get a full welcome with horns and cheering and loudspeakers announcing me. There are people everywhere.

My family is here. Mom sees the sled and her eyes go wide. Em hops up and down, screaming her head off. Dad is hooting and waving his fists in the air.

Guy is next to the trail preparing his dogs to come back for me. When he sees me, he laughs in relief. "Guy is impressed! But you stole his dogsled."

"It pulls a little to the right. You can have it back."

"Congratulations on completing the Great Superior Mail Run," one of the checkers says. "That's an unconventional finish, to say the least."

"Thank you. That's the way I roll."

I slide off the sled and go thank the dogs.

February 10, 2019

Attention: Foundation for Fighting Blindness

I am the mother of Emma Barney, who is eight years old and living with Stargardt disease. Emma has written to you using a special dogsled envelope to ask for a cure. If someone could please take the time to respond to this caring and brave little girl, I would be forever grateful. It would mean so much to my family if you could include some form of encouragement for her.

In addition, kindly direct me to the best contact for helping organize a Vision Walk fundraiser in my community this year.

Sincerely, Beth Barney

CHAPTER 34

I approach Guy's truck in the parking lot but don't see him.

I bite back my disappointment. I haven't seen him since this morning and I really wanted to talk with him again. We've spent the day here waiting for the rest of the teams to arrive. There's been a party-like atmosphere. The entire town of White River must have the day off to celebrate with us. There are so many people and so much noise, it makes it hard for me to find any one person. I hope I can meet up with Guy at the ceremony.

His gear rack is open at the back of the dog truck. There's a pair of binoculars hanging among the dog harnesses. Did he have that in his sled? Doing some birding along the way?

On his tailgate are a pair of boots, a rag, and shoe polish. It looks like someone had been weatherproofing them and stopped with the job half done. "Hello?" I call. No one is around.

Well, this is an opportunity too good to let pass. Quickly, I dip the rag in the can of black goop and coat the eyepieces of the binoculars. When he gets home, he'll have something to remember me by.

"McKenna!" Emma's voice.

I turn to see her standing there with her cane. She's alone. Not holding on to someone's arm, just standing tall by herself. My throat feels strange as I try to swallow.

"We're looking for you," she says. "Mom wants pictures with the dogs before all the awards and ceremonies start."

At the truck, I give my team a good rubdown while Mom snaps pictures. Each dog gets full attention and love and gratitude. I rub their backs and their shoulders, loosening the joints. I rub their butts and hamstrings. Sumo gets the biggest rubdown of all. He leans into me and lets himself slide down until his front elbow hooks on my knee.

"You're such a goof!" All he needs is a pair of shades and he'd make a great Instagram celebrity.

I move from dog to dog, all of them lolling their heads back and closing their eyes. I tell them all how brave they are, how much food they're going to get when we go home. How thick their beds will be with fresh straw. And how many more runs we'll do together. Because I'm never giving this up.

Boots crunching on snow behind me. I turn around. "They're starting in twenty minutes, McKenna," Dad says. "Sounds like all the teams are in now, and they've finished calculating the times."

At last, we'll find out who won. Em takes my arm with one hand, her cane in the other, and we walk toward the center together. We walk like that not because she has to, but because she wants to. The counselor had instructed her in how to use the cane. Em will have to practice more, learning things like when to tap and when to swipe, but it's a start. Dad's mouth is set in a grim line, but he doesn't say anything.

Once we're inside, we're directed to a table right next to the stage. It has a little placard on it. I hesitate a moment before using Em's magnifier to read it. RESERVED FOR BARNEY FAMILY.

I glance at my sister and then pull out a chair, pleased. It will be easier for Em to see what's going on from here. And then I realize that I can see the stage better too. Such a little thing to make life easier.

When we sit at the table, I look around at my family. I drink in the details of their faces because I don't know how long I'll be able to see them clearly. My throat tightens at the thought, but I blink it away. Right now, I can still see their faces. No one knows what the future holds.

And besides, Zesty has shown me that seeing is something you can do with your heart, not just your eyes.

By the time the room fills up with milling bodies and voices, the announcer is on the stage. "We'll begin by having all the mushers form a line at the side of the room there and deliver their mailbag to our postal representative, please."

I go over and stand in line along with everyone else, holding the mailbag that has made such an impact on my life. One by one, mushers hand their bags to the lady from the post office.

"Here you go," I say with pride. "Safe and sound. Delivered by dog team."

"That's the idea." She winks at me.

"And can I also give you this to put in the mail? It's from a friend of mine." I hand her Kelly's letter to her grandpa.

"Thank you. I'll make sure it goes in. Great job in the race."

When she takes the bag, I feel relief and loss in equal measures. Suddenly, I'm no longer a sworn mail carrier. But I managed to deliver the letters from Emma's whole class. I kept my promise. And I have some idea of how William Desjardins felt.

Wednesday, January 16, 2019

Dear students,

Surprise! Now you are the ones receiving an envelope with a "Delivered by Dog Team" stamp. And since you were such good letter writers, everyone wins one of these special dog-paw stickers, which were carried along the historic trail by sled dogs. You see, I told you getting mail is fun!

Love, Mrs. Wright

CHAPTER 35

O nce all the mushers find their seats again, the announcer goes back to the mike.

"Thank you, everyone. I hope you all enjoyed our first annual Great Superior Mail Run. It's been such a success, and we have you all to thank for that. We hope that you come back to race it next year. And tell your friends! Now, to the awards!"

Everyone cheers. My heart stutters.

"We're going to break with tradition and begin with first place. So, without further ado, after calculating all the times, we've arrived at our winner. A local from Sault Ste. Marie and one of our younger competitors, Guy Desjardins!"

Pure joy seizes me, and I hoot my head off. Someone stands up from the tables. I can't see who it is from here, but as he makes his way to the stage, I recognize Guy's walk. Another person, bulkier, also joins him onstage. Guy's dad, I assume, and it makes me so glad for him. The clapping in the room turns to laughter, though.

I look around quizzically. "What's going on?" I ask Mom, who's sitting beside me.

She's laughing too. She leans toward me and says, "For some reason, Guy has big black rings around his eyes, like a raccoon. That boy is strange."

I cringe. That wasn't supposed to happen till he left here. Especially not in front of all these people. But it *is* sort of perfect timing. I join in the laughter.

Guy stands in front of me onstage. He's wearing his old-timey mail uniform again, which would be really impressive, except his whole vibe is marred by what looks like an unfortunate encounter with a door.

I write the number one in the air above my head.

He points to me and laughs before accepting his award and the purse. Five thousand dollars for first prize will buy a lot of dog food. If his father's business doesn't get the Amazon contract, at least that money will help.

"I'd like to dedicate this win to my late Grandpa Desjardins.

And thanks to my dad for sponsoring me with his business, Desjardins Delivery. We are four generations of running dogs and running the mail!"

It's Guy's moment, and my heart swells to see him living it. There are reporters and media in the room snapping pictures and writing about what happens here. I hope they get his story right. And his black eyes just lend him an air of mystery that people can wonder about.

He struts by our table on his way back to his seat. When he's next to me, he pulls me up for a quick hug.

"I'm glad I met you," he says softly in my ear. He presses something into my hand.

His whisper makes my face flush. The skin on my neck bursts into goose bumps. I glance down and I don't need a magnifier to read the large-print phone number he's written.

"What?" I whisper. "We're not going to write *letters?*"

"There's this thing now called FaceTime. Try to keep up."

The next awards are being announced. Guy disappears, and I sit with a little smile.

Second and third place go to Marc Bondar and Bailey Gant, respectively. Even though I came in before her today, Bailey had a faster time yesterday. My added times probably put me in fourth place, but fourth place doesn't get a mention. I try not to let it bother me.

"The Red Lantern Award goes to Peyton Tomlinson. This award is to recognize the dedication it takes for being last and not giving up. We had a lot of mushers scratch during the storm, but some of you carried on, despite the challenges. Congratulations, Peyton."

A tall woman in the crowd stands and waves and then sits back down.

The announcer continues. "And by now, everyone must have heard about an unusual event that occurred near the end of the trail. The winner informs us that his win is due to one musher's selfless act of lending her sled. In doing so, she sacrificed her own race standings. This year's Sportsmanship Award goes to Mc-Kenna Barney!"

Em punches me in the arm. I stand and bow. I can hear Guy over the clapping in the room saying, "Way to go, Barney! That sounds like a good dog name!"

Mom looks at me proudly. Dad takes a picture and I feel so glad to be with them and not hiding.

The announcer onstage isn't finished. "And now for the last award of the night. Many will agree that this is the most important award in any dog race. And this year it goes to a very deserving musher. Her outstanding dog care shows in the fact that not only did she complete the full three legs of the race and deliver her mail, she also crossed the finish line with her entire team of dogs. McKenna Barney is deserving of the Humanitarian Award! Congratulations, McKenna. Come on up!"

I sit back, stunned. A cheer goes up around the room and Emma gives me a sideways hug. "Oh gosh, McKenna! I told you you'd be great!"

I've won both awards? The Sportsmanship Award is awesome. But the Humanitarian Award blows me away. This is the one that shows I look after my dogs. The dogs are the whole point, the reason I run. And to have recognition that I take care of my team is just the best feeling. I was so busy focused on the goal of winning, I forgot about the most important award of the race.

Mom and Dad are both looking at me with shiny eyes. I squeeze Em's hand and then find the strength to stand and move toward the stage on legs that feel like jelly.

When I get to the podium and look out at the roomful of mushers and handlers, friends and family and media, I can't see any individual faces. But I see the camera flashes going off. I raise a hand to block it, and I blink. All at once, an understanding hits me. I didn't need to deliver Emma's letter.

I *am* the letter.

"I ran this race for my sister," I begin. "It turned out I needed to run it for myself. I can see that now." I pause and then tell everyone, "But there isn't much I *can* see."

My heart feels as if it's going to burst right out of me. I've spent so long trying to fit in with everyone else and not be different. But I push on.

"I have trouble seeing anything in front of me lately. And I ran the whole race like that. But I've learned a lot." I step away from the podium so everyone can fully see me. I take a deep breath and then visualize Zesty charging ahead, refusing to have any barriers in her life.

"Let me tell you about something called Stargardt disease."

ACKNOWLEDGMENTS

I would like to thank the following people for helping me with the details of Stargardt disease and for taking the time to answer all of my questions: Sukanya Shankar, Cassidi Benavidez, Josephine Cimo Como, Bethany Richardson, Corinna Tanner, Trish Barsby, Andrea Chambers, Stela Trudeau, Harry Batten, and Florence Waddington. I so appreciate your sharing your personal stories.

Thank you to my sensitivity readers for wading through my manuscript: Denise O'Connor, Kristin Murner, Grace McMullin, and Andrea Chambers.

Thank you to my amazing editor, Ann Rider, and to Liz Agyemang for insightful suggestions and helping make the book so much better. I'm beyond grateful for your support and for sticking with me through a terrible year.

A huge thank you to my research assistant, Bruce Tomlinson, the most knowledgeable and patient historian I know, who continued feeding me sound advice even though I changed gears multiple times. Also thanks to Klaas Oswald for his help and local knowledge.

Thank you to Chris Barry of the Massey Area Museum for her time and enthusiasm. Thanks to Johanna Rowe and the Town of Wawa Heritage Committee. Thanks to the Smithsonian National Post Museum for the information in *Stories of the Klondike Gold Rush*. And to @wattleofbits for letting me use that great line.

And finally, thanks to my critique partners and beta readers. You know who you are and what you mean to me. Luckily, e-mails are faster than dog-team couriers.

AUTHOR'S NOTE

A sled-dog team in Michipicoten, Ontario, 1920. Photo courtesy of the Town of Wawa Heritage Committee.

This is a work of fiction, but many elements are based on historical events. The details in the letters from William Desjardins are all gleaned from the era of the dogsled mail couriers, from 1856 to the early 1900s. Raymond Miron and Eric Skead are actual men who ran the mail along the north shore, though the timeline has been altered to put them together in this story.

The White River Trail, the historical mail route between Pukaskwa Depot and White River, was well known. But it was difficult to find descriptions of the section between Sault Ste. Marie and Michipicoten beyond the mention of couriers running "the usual route." Therefore, to conjure the race route, I used a mix of research and local knowledge along with what the characters needed for dramatic purposes. For example, I fabricated a route running from Michipicoten that meets up with the White River Trail. The Pukaskwa checkpoint does not exist in real life. Pukaskwa Park is a large stretch of remote and beautiful wilderness without roads. The community center in Gargantua was created for the sake of the story, and the Cascades do exist but not where they appear on the trail before White River.

I visited the Ermatinger Clergue National Historic Site in Sault Ste. Marie, and the atmosphere and the Hudson's Bay Company roots of the museum resonated with me. I wanted to include it but had to take some liberties with the size of the room at Ermatinger House.

It has been challenging and rewarding writing a story set in northern Ontario, as this is where I've snowshoed and kayaked and hiked and mushed and explored. The inspiration for all of my books was born here. I hope to have done it justice.

ABOUT THE AUTHOR

TERRY LYNN JOHNSON lives at the edge of a lake in northern Ontario, Canada. For many years she was the owner and operator of a dogsledding business with eighteen huskies. She taught dogsledding at an outdoor school near Thunder Bay, Ontario. She has worked as a conservation officer with the Ontario Ministry of Natural Resources and Forestry for seventeen years. Before that, she worked for twelve years as a backcountry canoe ranger in Quetico Provincial Park, a large wilderness park in northwestern Ontario. In her free time, she enjoys snowshoeing and going on kayak expeditions with her husband. Her lifelong passion for adventure and wilderness continues to inspire her books.